Jairus's Girl

by

L. R. Hay

A Salted Lightly publication

www.saltedlightly.com

Cover design © Brian McGinnis, 2015

ISBN-13: 978-1519551788
ISBN-10: 1519551789

Jairus's Girl

The Young Testament

Galilee

For the aged parents

And the Aged Parent

With love   x

CONTENTS

Chapter	Page
1. A View from the Bushes	1
2. With Neighbours Like That...	9
3. Breakfast, Bread and Baby Brothers	16
4. Doing the Right Thing	26
5. The First Signs	34
6. When Nothingness Seems Best	40
7. The Man with the Nice Eyes	46
8. In the Cool of the Evening	52
9. The Law Turned on its Head	58
10. Dibs's Roof	66
11. Blessed Are the Percivals	73
12. A Brother At Last	79
13. Called to Follow, but Called to Stay	88
14. Intin... Itrin... Ite... Wandering Followers	94

15. Several Thousand into Five *Will* Go   100

16. Sorting Out the Squid   108

17. The Most Special Miracle   115

18. A Sky as Hard as Steel   123

19. All of Us, in Some Way   129

20. Shinier Than Your Average Gardener   136

21. He Definitely Did It   143

Chapter One

A VIEW FROM THE BUSHES

Once upon a time, as they say, a long while ago and in a country far, far from here (unless you happen to be reading this book somewhere like Turkey or Egypt, in which case it is really quite close), there was a thorn bush with a girl inside it. The girl's name was Tamar Bilkiah Keren Happuch Bath-Jairus. The thorn bush didn't have a name. Tamar Bilkiah Keren Happuch positively *hated* her name, so everyone called her Tammie. That is what I will call her from now on, and I suggest you do the same, or you'll still be reading this book in years and years - when you're at University, or training to be a juggler, or whatever it is you want to do.

Tammie wasn't usually in a thorn bush, but that is where she happened to be at the precise moment this story starts. She was playing Hide and Seek. It was one of her favourite games, though she pretended that she only played it for the sake of the little kids. Tammie was eleven; indeed she was as-nearly-as-anything-twelve, which is even older.

The reason Tammie liked it was that she was really very good at it. She would crawl somewhere no one would ever think of, very carefully, making sure that nothing was poking out like a foot, or a bit of her skirt. Then she would snuggle down and listen, and laugh to herself - but only an inside laugh. She even breathed really quietly. While the others in hiding got bored and started to fidget about, Tammie would just wait, and wait.

This time she'd managed to position herself so that she could see. There was Daniel, who was actually-properly-twelve. He was one of the ones who had drawn the straw to be on; unfortunately for him, the other was Jake. Daniel was very responsible and tried to do everything right, but Jakey (who was two) had only been allowed to play because he would scream if he was left out. He had demanded a piggy-back, and kept mountaineering about on Daniel's shoulders whenever he fancied a different view - stuffing his foot in Daniel's mouth, and occasionally falling off and dangling by his tunic - but in spite of all this, Daniel was trying his hardest to carry on with the game. The children were playing on a large area of wasteland close to Capernaum, which was where they lived, and as Daniel could hardly move, he had precious little chance of finding anyone.

He peered earnestly around, doing his best to see signs of movement or bright flashes of clothing - and every now and then he got someone. Whenever that happened, Jake would bellow "Whoop-di-diddly-dooya!!!" in his ear which, combined with the fact that he was often holding on by Daniel's hair, didn't really help. It was all very funny, and even more so because of the serious look on Daniel's face. Tammie found it quite hard not to giggle.

Even though it was early evening, the sun was shining down lovely and hot; just hot enough to make you glad of a little shade if you happened to be sitting inside a thorn bush. Capernaum was in Galilee in Northern Israel, a province of the Roman Empire at that time; it's at the blunt end of the Mediterranean if you want to find it on a map. Although at night in winter it could get really cold, and there was always the rainy season to wade through - sometimes literally - most of the time the weather was boiling hot, and very dry and dusty.

This sort of weather, thought Tammie lazily, was just right. It made her feel happy and sleepy and forget disagreeable things, like all the work she was supposed to do tomorrow. She could hear a flute playing gently over to her left, which was very soothing and made her want to yawn. She guessed that must be someone who was out and had gone to sit in the shade. It was a nice tune - not too lively, not too loud, but just the right sort of tune for the lazy end of a lovely day... Just the right sort of tune for falling asleep to, if you happened to be snuggled up in a quiet bush, with a warm breeze blowing the branches and a few inquisitive bees buzzing in to join you now and again.......

Suddenly there was an *enormous* sneeze. Daniel swung round as quickly as he could in the circumstances, and glared accusingly at a large clump of wild flowers and ferns.

"Dibs!" he shouted in triumph. (Whoop-di-diddly-dooya)

Dibs stood up in a sulk and flounced off to join the others, muttering to herself and anyone else who cared to listen that it wasn't fair, and sneezing shouldn't count, and it was a stupid game anyway, and she was bored. She looked very red in the face, as if she'd been holding that sneeze in for ages - and cross too, especially when everyone hooted and guffawed at her. Tammie nearly exploded, but it was just so typical of Dibs it really was impossible not to laugh. Fortunately the others were making such a noise that Daniel didn't notice a few random splutters from the thorn bush.

Dibs was Tammie's best friend. She was Jake's oldest sister, too - though sometimes she did behave so much like him (and pull her face just the same) that you might almost have thought she was his very tall twin. Her real name was Deborah, but when she was born and Tammie was a toddler, the nearest Tammie could get to pronouncing the name of the new baby was something that sounded like 'Dibbyral.' Deborah's mother had thought it was cute and suited her (which it still did, really), and it got changed and messed about with, and stuck at Dibs.

What was it the others had seen - was somebody coming? The chatter had died out, and several of the children were stumbling hurriedly into a shambolic line; even some in hiding stood up and guiltily brushed dust and dead grass from their clothes. It was obviously a grown-up, and one to be really respected - someone on their way home to Capernaum? Tammie bit her lip as she tried to squint round in the direction everyone was looking.

"No need to stop your game for me."

The rich voice rang out cheerfully, and Tammie hugged herself with glee. It was her father, back from yet another trip to Jerusalem. It was nice knowing how important he was, but nicer still when he came home again. She could see him now, and watched him laugh as those who had foolishly shown themselves disappeared again, and Daniel frantically tried to remember where they had been.

"You missed a few," Jairus said, "but I won't give them away. A beautiful evening. Has all been well here since I left?"

"Yes Rabbi," said Daniel - anxious to please, but nervous.

Jairus scanned the waste ground and his gaze rested on the thorn bush.

"Ah, there she is!" he grinned. "How long did it

4

take you to wriggle into there? I hope you were careful not to tear your dress."

"Of course I was," said Tammie, as she very, very carefully wriggled out again.

It was funny, though. Daniel, trying so hard, hadn't spotted her - but her father had. Not only picked up that flicker of light as her eyes glinted in the sunshine, but known it was her, right away. He was like that. He seemed to see things other people didn't; to know and understand really complicated things that nobody else could grasp. Tammie thought he was the cleverest, coolest person in the whole world.

She was free of the bush now, and ran towards him with all her might. She didn't feel sleepy anymore. All she wanted to do was get to him and give him the biggest hug ever. He picked her up and swung her round, then they looked at each other, laughing.

"I've spoilt your fun," he said.

"I don't care," she replied.

"Home then?"

"Yes, home."

And Tammie put her hand in his as they set off down the road.

Tammie's father was leader of the Synagogue in Capernaum where everybody went, especially on the Sabbath day, to worship God and be taught about him. It was a very important job; perhaps the most important there could be, apart from being a priest and serving at the Temple in Jerusalem, where the actual presence of God lived.

The people of Capernaum had great respect for Jairus. They often bowed to him in the streets or came to ask his advice, and they called him 'Rabbi', which means 'Master' or 'Teacher.' Tammie didn't call him that, of course. More often than not she would call him 'Abba.'

Your parents, if you asked them, would probably tell you that Abba was a 1970s Swedish pop group, who most people really rather liked at the time (don't tell anyone, but I've got one of their records).

You could then smile knowingly and say "Actually 'Abba' is an Aramaic word meaning a familiar form of 'Father'; for example, 'Daddy', 'Dad' or 'Poppa'." (But you had better check first that you know how to pronounce 'Aramaic', or you will spoil the whole effect)

Then they will probably say something like "Be quiet and eat your muesli," which will be their way of hiding how impressed they are by your great learning.

To Tammie, Aramaic was the natural language to speak; everyone at that time and in that part of the world spoke it. Some had learnt Hebrew as well, because that was the language of the writings about God in the Synagogue.

It is a curious part of human nature to want the opposite of what you have. Now, I would never dream of being so difficult, and I'm sure that you also would be far too pleasant and sensible - but I daresay you've noticed it in other people? Whatever they haven't got or can't do is *just* the thing they always wanted. Well, Tammie was absolutely not allowed to go to school. How many of us, when we are school age, would simply long for someone to tell us we can't come in? (Not you and me, of course - but other people) For Tammie it was a constant wish, and one that she was sure would put everything right, if only she could go to the school.

School in Capernaum a long time ago was very different. They had no Maths, or Earth Sciences, or P.E.

(I bet you just wish you lived then, don't you? No, of course you don't; I was forgetting). Tammie couldn't go because it was only for boys, and from the age of six they began to learn Hebrew and remember chunks of the Holy writings. Boys and girls would also learn practical skills like fishing, spinning and weaving, cooking or carpentry - but they got these from their parents. School was only for learning from the Rabbi about God and the history of the Jewish people.

Of course, Tammie was lucky that her father *was* the Rabbi, so she would pester him to teach her things. She wasn't as keen on getting the Hebrew right as Jairus would have wished; she had a very creative approach to spelling and grammar. But her love of hearing stories from the scrolls in the Synagogue (what we might call the Old Testament, or Mikra) was as great as Jairus's love of telling them. They could often be seen strolling together, by the lake or in the countryside, through fields or olive groves, deep in conversation. They would talk of famous people from the Bible, like Solomon or Moses, Esther or Jacob, as if these people were living just round the corner. They talked of God in that way, too; as if he were someone who had just nipped out, but if you cared to hang around he was bound to be back pretty soon.

Tammie used to think about God quite a bit. She wondered what he looked like, and was impatient that she couldn't see him. The glory of God was just too great for a human to bear, Tammie knew that, but she often wished it could be different.

This evening, daughter and dad were talking of all sorts of things as they walked home to Capernaum. Jairus was telling of his trip to Jerusalem to meet with the other leaders on the big Council, and teasing her by

7

saying he had brought a present but not telling her what it was. Then Tammie was telling him about everything that had happened since he went, and especially how Dibs had flicked an orange onto a tall cupboard, which wasn't quite as stupid as it sounds because they had been pretending to be the shepherd boy David killing the giant Goliath with a stone and a catapult thing, so obviously the cupboard had been the giant but Dibs had aimed a bit high, and they had stood on stools to try to get the orange back, because it was the only one they had at the time and they were planning on sharing it, and the cupboard had overbalanced, and Tammie's mother had come in an hour later to find them pinned to Tammie's bed by a cupboard, but at least they did get the orange back - a bit bruised - the orange, not them - well actually, them as well - but it tasted every bit as nice, which was a good thing because they both got pretty hungry while they were stuck under the cupboard......

Chapter Two

WITH NEIGHBOURS LIKE THAT...

Jairus was not skipping and hopping about and talking in long sentences and getting out of breath like Tammie, but he must have been tired too. His journey from Jerusalem had taken a few days. A small group of Rabbis from nearby towns had gone, with some servants and assistants. They had taken donkeys to ride when they wanted, and to carry the baggage. That had made it a quicker journey, but Jairus felt he had been away from his people far too long. Everyone had split up on this last day to go to their own places, and Jairus had let his companions Caleb and Benjamin take the donkeys on ahead while he found Tammie.

They walked down the hill towards the lake, sparkling into the distance. It was called the Sea of Galilee, because it was more like a little sea than a big lake. The town of Capernaum was sort of snuggled on the northern shore, and very pretty it looked in the golden, rosy light of the evening. From higher up the hill they had been able to see one or two fishing boats on their way home from the middle of the water - and, quite hazily, a few miles further along the edge, Bethsaida, the nearest town to them. But now they were much closer; the rest of the view had fallen away and Capernaum was right in front of them.

It was a very small sort of town. Tammie knew that Jerusalem was much bigger, because she had been there a few times. The nicest building was the Synagogue; no town nearby had one as beautiful as this. It was new, and built more in the Roman style - simple and clean-cut, with pillars and carved panels. It had all been paid for by Marcellus, the officer in charge of the Roman soldiers posted in the nearby fort, when the old Synagogue had become too ramshackle. The people of Capernaum were very proud of their Synagogue.

The houses were arranged along streets of flattened earth, and were mostly squarish with flat roofs. Some were big, some small - some new, some old - but they were nearly all made from big blocks of basalt, the local stone, and they had pretty nifty ways of keeping cool. Many were painted pale colours to reflect away the sun. Some had big doors the whole length of one side, which could be opened up as if a wall were missing. Quite a few had a staircase or ladder going up to the flat roof; when the sun wasn't too scorching people would go up there to have a meal or do their work. On summer nights they could even sleep on the roof, rolling themselves up in a blanket under the stars.

It was a pleasant little place to live in; just an ordinary fishing town, like so many others; never very busy, nothing much ever happening. Tammie didn't know of anywhere else she would rather be.

Tammie's home was the first you came to as you walked down the hill. It was set back from the houses near it, high enough on the slope to have a lovely view over the rest of the town and down to the lake. A big house compared to many, built around a courtyard, but not too big to seem welcoming and homely. The walls were a creamy white, though at the moment tinted with the colours of the sun which would soon be setting. At one side were a few trees, - olives and acacias, with droopy branches. The lush green leaves made you feel cool just looking at them, and contrasted with the white of the house.

The gates of the archway stood open just now. Tammie could see the donkeys being unloaded in the courtyard while a crowd of townspeople fussed around looking busy, taking bags inside and bringing buckets out to fill at the well and give to the donkeys. The donkeys were far too interested in the food and water to stand in convenient places for the people unloading them, so the people unloading were getting heated with the ones doing the feeding and watering, and things could have been done a great deal more quickly with a great deal fewer people.

That was often the case. Because Jairus was the Rabbi they always had people from the town popping round to give a hand, when they could manage perfectly well - particularly as they had Rachel, Caleb and Benjamin living with them to help with the work.

A lot of people did it for the best reasons; Jairus was popular, and it was natural that they should want to thank him. But there were others, Tammie suspected, who did it so they could boast that they were friends with the Rabbi's family - and even to show off to the Rabbi how good they were. She heartily wished they would all go away now, because her father was tired and had been away for weeks.

No chance of that yet, though. The minute they saw Jairus, people left their jobs and thronged round him, shaking his hand, welcoming him home and inquiring after his health, the journey, the meetings in Jerusalem and so on. He spoke to them kindly, thanking them for their trouble, but couldn't help looking around a bit. It was obvious who he really wanted to see.

There she was in the courtyard, Tammie's mother Naomi, looking slightly more flustered than usual as she went around the extra helpers with a tray of cool fruit drinks. She was talking to people too, and putting them at their ease, but like Jairus her mind was only half on it. She had seen him through the open gates and wanted to go to him. Tammie pushed round the outside of the crowd and into the yard, coming up alongside her mother and taking the tray.

"I'll do this. Go and see Daddy!"

Naomi didn't need persuading but slipped out, drying her hands on her apron and trying to catch back one or two odd strands of hair that had escaped from the rest in all the confusion. As Tammie peered through all the people she could just see her father put his arm round Naomi and give her a polite squeeze. He couldn't really give her a big sloppy kiss in front of the others, Tammie supposed, but she rather wished he would. That might shake them up a bit.

Rachel came out of the house with another trayful of drinks, puffing and complaining about the heat. She was big and cuddly, and now she was getting on a bit in age the weather always made her short of breath. She usually pretended to be cross as well, but that was just her joshing.

"He's back then, I see," she commented to Tammie, dumping the tray on a jutting out bit of wall and setting off to collect empty cups from where they had been abandoned. You wouldn't catch Rachel swanning round, handing out drinks and making social chit-chat. The whole thing was looking more like a cocktail party every minute.

"Your help has been invaluable; I think we're straight now," said Naomi to the crowd in her tactful way. "You really are most kind and thoughtful." That was the nearest to a hint to get rid of them she was likely to give. It didn't work.

"Meddlers and gossips," muttered Rachel as she went past Tammie with her arms full, on her way back to the kitchen. "There's jugs for a top-up when they've got through that lot. I'm washing these cups or we won't have enough. Don't let her offer them food, or we'll be here all night."

"Sssh, someone will hear you!" said Tammie.

"Oh, they know me."

"Smile, Rachel. Isn't it worth it to have Daddy back?"

"I daresay it would be, if he was my daddy."

"Go along, old Moody Kecks. You're nearly as fond of him as I am."

"Go along yourself," retorted Rachel, disappearing.

Finally the drinks were gone and there were obviously no more on the way, so people drifted off. Tammie gave a huge sigh, and Jairus laughed and gave his wife a proper hug and a kiss.

"Amazing how many people it takes to unload a few donkeys," said Benjamin. "Can't think how we managed when we arrived in Jerusalem."

"Amazing how much drink it takes, too," said Caleb.

The two of them had been sitting in a corner of the yard, ignored by the eager helpers, enjoying a rest and supper. Caleb, by far the older, took the opportunity to remove his sandals and massage his aching feet now that there were only family present, so to speak. Caleb had been with them much longer than Tammie, or even Naomi; he had worked for Jairus's dad when Jairus was a little boy, and to Tammie he was almost like a grandfather.

"We can go straight in, I think," said Naomi. "The

13

donkeys are in the stable, and the bags have been carried inside and put away."

"In all the wrong places," came a disembodied voice from the kitchen.

"Ah, Rachel!" said Jairus. "I was wondering when I would be swamped by your welcome."

Rachel's head appeared at the window. "Haven't you had enough welcomes for one night?"

"I want yours."

"Welcome home," she said, without changing the sour expression on her face, and disappearing again immediately.

"It's good to know that some things never change," said Jairus, stretching and yawning. "How are things here? Nothing's happened since I went?"

"No, everything is pretty much the same," said Naomi. "The fever has spread. Lucius has it now; you know, that servant of Marcellus the centurion."

"Marcellus must be gutted," said Benjamin. "He's too soft-hearted to be a Roman officer."

"He's a good man," said Jairus. "I might speak to him tomorrow; he deserves any help we can offer. Most Roman soldiers ill-treat the people they're set to govern. What about Old Sarah, is she no better?"

"No," sighed Naomi. "Her fever's worse. She's getting weaker and weaker; I suppose we shouldn't be surprised, at her age."

"I'm going to see her tomorrow, when I take the food," said Tammie, holding her father's arm and swinging on it like Jake had sometimes done with Daniel in the game earlier on.

"She probably won't recognise you, darling, so don't be upset," said Naomi. "She's not known me the last couple of times. Poor Old Sarah."

"What's all this 'old'?" said Rachel, emerging unexpectedly into the courtyard. "She's only a few years older than me. And what are you lot doing talking out here, when you could be having a rest inside?" She eyeballed Jairus. "I've put your supper inside; for goodness sake go and sit down." Then she added suddenly, "It's good to see you back," as if by saying it quickly no one would notice that she was being nice.

"It's good to be back. It really is," he replied, giving her a squeeze.

"Foreign manners," she said with a sniff.

"I've only been to Jerusalem," he said.

"Judean manners, then; that's worse. Get in. You look after him," she said to Tammie and Naomi, "and I'll take these two. Though I think you've got the best of the deal."

They all made their way inside. As Rachel, Caleb and Benjamin went up the corridor they could hear them arguing all the way. Rachel started it, of course, attacking Caleb who was carrying his sandals in his hand:

"You're not thinking of taking your feet into my kitchen?"

"Well I wasn't thinking of leaving 'em outside."

"They smell."

"Good. With a bit of luck they'll drown out the smell of your cooking."

Jairus put an arm each round Naomi and Tammie and gave them both a kiss.

"It really is good to be home."

Chapter Three

BREAKFAST, BREAD AND BABY BROTHERS

When Tammie woke the next morning the first thing she saw was the gift her father had brought her. She smiled to herself because Jairus was home, and slid out of bed, taking the present across to the small hole in the wall that acted like a window. Opening the wooden shutter, she held it up in the sunlight. It was even more beautiful than she had thought last night, in the odd, flickery light of the oil lamps: a wide belt of plaited silk in midnight blue, shot through with streaks of crimson and purple. The clasp was beaten silver, and Tammie had never been given anything so precious.

Most of her clothes were linen rather than the rougher wool or goat's hair, but even the finest didn't feel like this. It was just the right colour, too; her best dress was pale blue. Tammie sighed as she ran the luscious silk through her fingers. She wished it was Shabbat, the Sabbath day, which God had given them each week to rest; she could have worn the belt without spoiling it. But she would just have to hang it up again, and put on some work clothes.

Tammie decided to eat her breakfast in her special corner up on the roof, with the sun warming her face a little. It was still very early, and the only time of day that was really cool in this part of the year. It was refreshing up there, and when you'd had enough of eating you could kneel up and watch the birds in the branches of the trees right next to you, or look out over Capernaum and see people beginning to stir about (and see whether the shutter to Dibs's bedroom was open yet, which it usually wasn't) - or confuse the chickens down in the courtyard by throwing some corn, then watch them looking all round to see who had thrown it.

Tammie ate her breakfast slowly. She had helped herself to a bowl of yoghurt with honey dribbled on it, which was her favourite, and a chunk of bread to dip in it. She was actually looking forward to the work planned for today. Once a week for some time now, Tammie's mother had made extra food for Old Sarah's family, so that Rebekah, her daughter, would be able to get her washing done. As Rebekah had three small children to look after, and her husband Simon was always working hard, Sarah's illness had made things difficult for them. Sometimes Tammie had gone with Naomi to take the food, but today for the first time she was going by herself, as Naomi would be busy dealing with all the baggage from the Jerusalem trip.

Tammie licked the empty bowl, then stretched out with satisfaction. She heard someone moving around in the courtyard and peered over the edge. There was her mother, shading her eyes to look up at her.

"Morning! Had your breakfast?"

"Yes, thanks," Tammie called back.

"That explains it. I thought there was a little less yoghurt in the bowl and a lot more honey on the floor."

Tammie grinned; Naomi was only winding her up because she knew exactly what she would pick if she made her own breakfast.

"Actually, it's a lot less yoghurt in the bowl, not a little," said Tammie.

"I suppose we should be grateful if there's any left at all."

Tammie went down to join her mother, and they began the day's jobs. Rachel and Benjamin unpacked the baggage and sorted it into piles: things to wash; things to put away; things to bury until they stopped being radioactive. (Joke. Though Rachel did threaten to burn Caleb's travel sandals) Caleb tended the animals they kept - chickens, donkeys and a few sheep; they didn't have many, because they lived on the things given to the Rabbi as a sort of wage. Jairus set off to see a few people, and then to teach the boys of the town as he did every day. Tammie would have to wait till evening to talk with him again.

Naomi and Tammie sat together on some steps in the courtyard and prepared huge piles of vegetables for a stew. That finished, they took them into the kitchen and put them in the big cooking pot. The meat smelled good bubbling gently in the water, slowly cooking to make it tender. Then Tammie scrubbed her hands and wiped her eyes which had been got at by the onions, because now it was time to make some bread, and hopefully some cake too.

Have you ever made bread? Tammie loved it. It was such good fun squishing your fingers around in the warm gooey paste, and then punching away like mad when you'd got it into a dough. Making bread is a good excuse to get your hands remarkably messy without anyone being upset (providing you haven't got the kitchen/your clothes/the cat/the family silver, jewels or artworks/your elderly relatives remarkably messy as well; that's the trick to remember for the 'no one getting upset' bit).

Making cakes, on the other hand, is a good excuse to eat the creamy stuff left in the bowl when it's been poured out, and that's what Tammie did as she sat resting at midday, waiting for the others to gather for the light meal they had at this time.

After lunch, Tammie set out for Rebekah's house. She carried a big basket which slowed her down, although she was used to lugging heavy things around. In it was a huge covered bowl of stew, several loaves, a cake and a smaller bowl with broth for Old Sarah, full of nourishment.

Tammie trudged through the town, saying hello to people as she passed. The door to Dibs's house was open, so Tammie looked in and was greeted by the very elegant sight of Dibs's rear end sticking up, covered in an enormous apron which seemed to engulf all of Dibs except her head and arms. She was on her hands and knees scrubbing the stone floor, awash with water and soap suds. Having her back (or rather, her bottom) to the door, she wouldn't have noticed Tammie, if it hadn't been for Jake who was tied to her waist by a rope. She was supposed to be minding her little brother as well as cleaning the floor, and anyone who'd had to mind Jake knew it was impossible even if you had nothing else to do. Dibs had tied him to her, in the futile hope of keeping him out of mischief. He now saw Tammie standing in the doorway and set off towards her, shouting in great excitement. Dibs made a desperate grab for the floor but couldn't stop herself sliding on all the water. She was dragged along helplessly, before finally managing to stand up; then she reined Jake in a bit more tightly and tried to rub the soap bubbles from her face.

Tammie had lots to tell Dibs about her father's return. While they were talking, Jake kept them nicely entertained; standing perfectly still and pretending to be a very good boy, then suddenly darting away and pulling Dibs off balance, or running round and round her trying to tie her up (and usually succeeding), narrowly missing the bucket more times than was comfortable.

That was another example of wanting the opposite of what you've got. Tammie had no brothers or sisters and she used to long for some with all her heart, even when she saw the minor inconveniences. If you are an only child too, you've probably felt how lovely it would be to have brothers and sisters to play with; to plan escapades, share jokes and generally have an excellent time. If, on the other hand, like Dibs you have brothers or sisters (Dibs had thousands, - OK, loads - OK, six - all younger than her) I suppose you might well long to have no one to scribble on your books, no one to jump on your stomach first thing in the morning, and no one to play aeroplanes very loudly when you are having a nice quiet time with your mother.

When they'd finished their chat, Tammie untangled Dibs once more and went on her way - hearing the wails of Jake as she left, and Dibs's threats to put the bucket over his head if he didn't stop it. Maybe it was quite nice to be able to walk away from other people's baby brothers.

It seemed a long walk to Simon and Rebekah's, right down at the edge of the lake, and Tammie's hands were thinking about the odd blister. She felt like another break as she got near the home of her mother's friend Salome, so she put down her basket and peered in from a short distance.

Salome must have seen her; she came to the door and sat on the piece of wall that was her usual place to watch the world go by, so that they could talk. Tammie always wanted to give Salome a big hug, but that was the one thing she couldn't do. No one was allowed to go anywhere near her, or even enter her house.

Salome had been ill for many years, since within a few weeks of Tammie being born, in fact - and for this sort of illness God's laws said that the person should be declared 'unclean'. This didn't mean that Salome was a dirty person, just that her illness might affect others. No one could touch her, or anything she had touched, because then they would become 'unclean' as well. Tammie was sorry for Salome with all her heart for the lonely life she had.

"How are you feeling today?" she asked.

"Not too good," smiled Salome blearily.

"Are you eating properly?" enquired Tammie, in a very grown-up way. That was the right thing to ask people who were poorly, she knew. Preferably with a stern look, and a shake of the head.

"Well,... " Salome hesitated in a way that made Tammie suspect the answer was no; "I'm trying to keep my strength up."

Tammie didn't want to be nosey, but this didn't sound right. What would be the best thing to say next? Yes, that was it.

"Lots of meat? Plenty of fish, and... and pulses," she couldn't remember what they were, but it sounded good; "and nice healthy vegetables?"

"Well, they do cost rather a lot, my dear; and I'm not up to growing my own vegetables, you know."

Tammie sat down on a step and gazed across the road at Salome, feeling even more alarmed. She didn't try to think of anything grown-up this time, but instead launched into a topic most adults would do a great deal to avoid.

"But I thought you had lots of money? My Daddy always said we should thank God that even though you couldn't work, you would always be comfortable!"

"It's gone. You can't keep seeing all those doctors, each with their bills to be paid, and each promising you a cure in just a few more months, without it eating away at your savings." She looked at Tammie very earnestly. "I wouldn't have minded, as long as at the end of it I had got back my health. Money's nothing compared to that. But as things are, my strength is still draining away, and I have nothing to live on. What can I do? How will I earn a living? Nobody can touch anything I've touched!"

"We will take care of you! You have no need to worry while we are here."

"Oh, I know that my dear, but that isn't the point. I will have to be dependent on people's kindness for the rest of my life. I'm already imprisoned in this house; now I've even lost the freedom of providing for myself. It's difficult to explain, but it meant a lot; it was the only thing of myself I had left."

Tammie jumped up, as an idea occurred to her.

"Would you like some stew?" she asked. "There's lots, and Mummy would want you to have it if she knew."

"She would, I'm sure. I've been working up the courage to tell her what state I'm in, but it's not an easy thing to come out and say - and she doesn't ask such direct questions as you. Yes, I'll take a little stew if you can spare it."

Tammie left a bowl where she could come out and fetch it, and then she took her leave, blowing Salome a kiss from across the road.

Further up the street she had to pass someone else who was considered 'unclean', although for very different reasons. Matthew, the tax collector, was sitting as usual at the booth where he collected money for the Romans - plus as much extra for himself as he wanted. If someone wouldn't pay whatever he demanded, he could get the Roman soldiers to force them. Tammie kept her eyes to the ground and hoped he wouldn't speak to her.

She glimpsed a slight movement from the corner of her eye, and the next second a shower of pebbles rained down on Matthew's head. He leaped to his feet and swung round angrily, roaring at the top of his voice at the handful of boys who were scuttling out of sight across the rooftops, laughing and calling names.

Tammie jumped at the sound of Matthew's shout, and sped up as much as she could without breaking into a run. Matthew slumped back into his chair, chuntering to himself. One of the boys had definitely been Dibs's brother Joel, but he knew it was pointless complaining. The boys' fathers would be delighted to hear what their lads had done; they might even have suggested it.

Matthew glowered at Tammie as she hurried past, as far from him as she could get. He knew exactly what she was thinking; all the people of Capernaum felt the same. They hated men like Matthew more than they hated the Romans. Not a Roman himself, but despised by his own people, Matthew was rich but belonged nowhere. He was probably as lonely in his 'uncleanness' as Salome, but the good people of Capernaum cared nothing for that.

Tammie kept her eyes steadfastly down until she had got well past him, and left him totting up the money in his books. She was on the last leg of her journey now, rounding the corner onto the shore of Galilee. She loved that sudden view across the lake, the water so close, and stretching on and on into the haze. She breathed in really deep, as if the air were somehow purer here next to the lake. Various people were scattered along the shore; fishermen mostly, and some children. Capernaum had the usual mixture of jobs, but fishing was the main business and if you didn't like fish there wouldn't have been much you could do about it. A fishy smell hung over the whole plaice (sorry, place) - and if that sounds gross, you must remember that to them it was normal. I dare say *they'd* have gone "bleaaaaruuuwoooghh!" at the thought of living in a town with factories, lorries and cars. (That 'bleaaaaruuuwoooghh' was a word I just made up. It's pronounced 'bleaaaaruuuwoooghh.' I may make up some more words, to keep you on your toes)

Tammie walked towards Rebekah's house, feeling excited at doing this job all by herself. No one would be in, except Old Sarah. Simon and his brother Andrew would be off working in their boat, and Rebekah would be out of town, up on the banks of the stream, doing the washing with her children. They were too dinky to help, but she would have taken them to keep an eye on them. Sarah used to do that, before she became ill. All the fisher children, and many others, loved Old Sarah and had often been minded by her when they were toddlers. She had always lived there, and everyone knew her. There had been many times when she had looked after grown-ups, too; whenever there was illness she was there, tending the sick person and praying for them. It seemed so wrong that now she had a fever herself. Being old it had taken her badly, and no one expected her to be around much longer. But Sarah was always a great one for common sense; she would have said that the important thing was to help Simon and Rebekah, and that is just what Tammie intended to do.

She opened the door, waving to Daniel who was on the shore sorting a new catch of fish with his father, Zebedee, and then she went inside - into the cool dimness of the house.

Chapter Four

DOING THE RIGHT THING

Tammie had been to the house a few times with her mother, so she knew just what to do. The first thing was to peep into Sarah's room to check that she was all right. The door was a little open for air to pass through; there she was, lying on her padded mat, looking feverish. Her breathing was heavy and hoarse, and Tammie could see that she was sweating a lot. Whether she was asleep or unconscious Tammie couldn't tell, but if it was sleep it didn't seem to be the healthy, refreshing kind. When Tammie had gone before, Sarah had been able to talk a little and smile at them weakly from her bed, but she had got worse since then. This was what Tammie had been expecting, so she just turned to get on with her work, trying not to be sad.

The afternoon went well. Naomi had told her just to concentrate on the main things, but Tammie decided she would do it all - partly because she wanted to help Rebekah, and partly just for the fun of knowing she could. She made up and lit the fire, and put the stew into the big pot to finish cooking. Then she put the bread and cake away. That was a mistake, as there were one or two little lemon cakes in the cubby hole, and Tammie loved lemon cakes. The thought of them sitting there kept plaguing her.

After that she busied herself with drawing water, cleaning and tidying, and seeing to anything Rebekah hadn't had time to do that morning. The main room was a sort of kitchen, dining room, sitting room and bedroom combined. It was nice and big, with a large doorway that looked right over the lake.

Suddenly a noise cut through the stillness and made Tammie start; it was Sarah. She ran to the door and looked in. The old woman was thrashing around restlessly, violently, crying out in her fever. Tammie stood there frozen for a moment, not knowing what to do, then she ran round to the neighbours' houses to find help. No one was in the first, or the next one, and it was quite a few along before Tammie found anyone. There was a woman she didn't know very well, sitting at the door of her house, doing her washing up in a tub.

Tammie breathlessly explained what had happened and asked her to come quickly, but the woman didn't move. She squinted up at Tammie against the sunshine, and asked what she expected her to do about it. Tammie was surprised and thought she mustn't have understood, so she repeated it.

"Please, you must come at once! Old Sarah needs help, and I don't know what to do."

"What makes you think I do?" asked the woman calmly, carrying on with her work. "She's got a fever and she's dying - there's no help anyone can give her."

"Surely we could at least make her more comfortable?"

"What's the point? She'll be gone soon anyway. All's we could do is catch it ourselves. It's her family's job, let them take the risk. Nothing to do with us."

"She wouldn't have said that," burst out Tammie in desperation. "She was always looking after people who were ill."

"More fool her," replied the woman. "That's probably how she got it in the first place."

Tammie gave up and rushed back to the house. She stood at the door helplessly and watched Sarah fight for breath against the greater force of the fever. It was unbearable to see such a kind, gentle woman struggling like this.

Tammie had been warned never to go into Sarah's room because of the danger of catching the illness, but as she stood there she tried to think what her father or mother would do. That woman's point of view was probably sensible, but Tammie wasn't sure it was good. Even if Old Sarah was going to die, that didn't make it all right not to care about her. As for the danger, Tammie *was* afraid, but her fear didn't change things. Above all else, she knew what Old Sarah would do: whatever she thought was right, and trust God to sort out the rest. Tammie walked into the room and sat on the floor next to the mat.

She mopped up the sweat from Sarah's face, then wondered what to do next. It was pointless, really; she hadn't a clue how to treat someone so ill. She took the old woman's wrinkled hand and started stroking it, as if soothing an animal or a crying child. That gave her an idea. She remembered being very little, and sitting on Sarah's knee. She remembered the songs of the fisherfolk that Sarah used to sing to her; comic songs that made her laugh, adventurous tales she would listen to wide-eyed, and the lullabies - as soft and lilting as being rocked in a boat on the calm lake. She could remember so clearly now the warmth of Sarah's lap, the slight lulling motion of her rocking chair, and the low, old voice singing those beautiful songs that would stop her tears and send her drifting off to sleep.

Tammie began to sing one of those lullabies, haltingly at first as she tried to remember the words, still stroking Sarah's hand and wiping the drops from her forehead. After a little while it seemed to be soothing her, and in time Sarah settled and lay calmly, just whimpering a bit. Tammie waited until she was sure Sarah would not miss her, then slipped quietly out of the room.

Looking through the open door towards the lake, Tammie saw that Simon and Andrew's boat had landed and they were sorting their catch, spreading the nets on drying frames to clean them. They would be home fairly soon, so Tammie put a pot of water on the fire for them to have a good wash. She was feeling rather nervous now; this was the part of the day she had not been looking forward to.

Basically, she was scared of Simon. She would never have admitted it, but that was what it was. When she saw him playing with his children or singing to God in the Synagogue she wondered why she was so silly, as he seemed quite a decent sort of man. But he was absurdly tall and solid; nowadays we would say he looked like the baddie from an action movie (if any superhero ever had a fisherman as their arch nemesis) - and he hardly ever spoke. He seemed gruff, too; Tammie always felt that he was going to shout at her, though he never had in her life. When she had confided this to her mother once, Naomi had laughed.

"Has it never occurred to you that perhaps he may be shy too?" she said, but Tammie couldn't believe that. Why on earth would a grown-up be shy?

Simon and Andrew were walking towards the house now, and Tammie started to panic and look for something to be doing when they came in. They were discussing something, and as they got near Andrew broke away and went off. He was probably going to carry the laundry back for Rebekah.

Oh, terrific. That was just about the worst thing that

could have happened. Now there would be just the two of them, not saying anything and getting more and more awkward. Nothing but a huge deafening silence.

Simon entered the house and nodded to Tammie in a grim sort of way. She gulped a little but couldn't get rid of the lump in her throat to say hello, so just nodded back with a simpering sort of smile. A flying start. He went to check on Sarah, so Tammie rushed to pour the hot water into the washing bowl and neatly folded a towel with the soap next to it. Hopefully he wouldn't think she was a *total* doofus. Then she tried to occupy herself and look useful, fiddling and tidying, and re-doing jobs she had done earlier on.

He came back and gave his hands a good scrub. Tammie wished her mother was there. Naomi always knew what to say, and could make the most uptight person comfortable immediately. Even Simon would become talkative by comparison. He was towelling himself dry now, wandering over to look at the stew.

"Smells good," he commented.

This was just plain silly; there must be *something* she could say.

"There's broth for Sarah," she ventured, slightly higher than usual. That hadn't been too bad, although it was rather obvious since he was looking right at it.

He lifted it from the fire, wrapping the towel round the handle, so Tammie hastily fetched a bowl and spoon, doing a slight juggling act as she nearly dropped them. Simon poured the broth in, saving some for the baby, then went to feed Sarah. Tammie drifted to the door and watched.

It was curious to see him trying to be careful as he sat her up a little and began feeding her so patiently. He looked as if he were feeding the baby: a small spoonful at a time, and watch out for any dribbles. The rough, strong hands seemed gentle, if a little clumsy. Tammie couldn't help a few tears running down her cheek, though she didn't exactly know why.

She was surprised to see when Simon turned round that he had tears in his eyes too.

"She was a good woman," he said.

As he came back into the main room, Tammie plucked up courage to speak again.

"Do you think there's any chance? That she'll get better, I mean."

He shook his head.

"Won't be much longer."

Although they didn't speak again, Tammie felt more at home now. When she had finally got everything nice for Rebekah she went and fetched her basket.

Simon put a squashy parcel of fresh fish into it, without a word. He often brought a gift like that to the Rabbi; he would leave it inside the gate and knock on one of the shutters. You would only know it was him if you ran out quickly and managed to catch a glimpse of his big, burly figure disappearing along the streets.

As Tammie went to the door, he said "You've worked hard," and handed her a lemon cake. Tammie couldn't help her face lighting up. He gave a little laugh, as if he had guessed they were on her mind.

She went out blinking into the sunlight, on her way home with her teeth sunk into the cake. Part way through the town she bumped into Simon's brother Andrew, carrying an enormous soggy bundle of wet washing, and Rebekah, carrying a smaller soggy bundle of wet baby. The other two little ones were running around, chuckling and gurgling and tripping up the adults. Rebekah had obviously let them play in the stream; they were both soaking wet and the water was turning to steam in the warmth of the sun. They thought it was hysterically funny, squelching all around, and Tammie had to laugh to see them. She knew that whenever Rebekah gave them a bath they screamed and tried to get away.

Tammie peered at the baby, in the way people always do. There wasn't much point cooing at him as he was asleep, so she just said "Aah" and left it at that. He was sleeping with one thumb in his mouth and the other in his ear; if those old-fashioned telephones had been invented he would have looked like a chubby, bald businessman making a call - but as they hadn't been, he didn't. The traditional drooling over the baby finished, she left them to take the steaming toddlers back to their dad and gran, and rushed home.

The first thing that greeted her was a very familiar smell - the stew. After helping to make it such an age ago (that morning, in fact), then lugging it for miles and miles (to the other side of town) and then being tantalised by the smell for all eternity (well, all afternoon), at last she was going to eat it. No amount of lemon cakes could have stopped her being ravenous. She rushed into the courtyard, flung the basket, fish and all, into Rachel's lap, and hurled herself at her father.

Her timing was perfect, as everyone was ready for the meal. Huge bowlfuls were dished out, with a loaf in the middle to help yourself to, and jugs of weakened wine and fruit juices. Everyone found somewhere comfortable to sit around the courtyard, then Jairus thanked God for giving them the food and good company to eat it with (which Tammie said a hearty 'Amen' to, on both counts), and they all tucked in.

They chatted as they ate - telling of the day's experiences, and anything else that came to mind. When they had eaten their fill, they carried on talking in a lazier way; enjoying the cool of the evening and the beautiful red sunset that meant another fine day tomorrow.

After a while Rachel, Caleb and Benjamin went inside, but Tammie stayed out with her parents watching the first few stars appearing. It was late for her to be up, but no one minded so soon after her father's return (they usually timed going to bed and getting up to fit in with sunset and sunrise, which is very sensible if you have no electric lights). Tammie snuggled up next to her mother and father, listening to them talk and reflecting on the success of the day - and particularly how very mature she had been getting over that silly shyness she used to feel with some grown-ups when she was much younger. Last week, in fact.

Chapter Five

THE FIRST SIGNS

It was a few days before Tammie noticed there was anything wrong. It must be the sun, she thought. She was with her mother, Rachel and Dibs and other women from the town, up on the banks of the Korazin - the stream that flowed down from the mountains and into the Sca of Galilee.

Of all the work that had to be done, cleaning the laundry was the only one that Tammie really did *not* like. It might sound like an exotic holiday to be standing in the sun with your feet in the silky, cool water of the stream, but when you actually tried it for a few hours it wasn't so romantic. For one thing, there weren't enough trees along the banks to give everyone shade, so now and then you would have to take a turn in the full sunshine, which beat down on the back of your head. Also you had to stoop down to the water to scrub the clothes, which made your back ache.

When your feet were pretty much numb enough to shrivel up like a raisin and drop off, you could get out and kneel on the bank, which thankfully meant you had less far to lean over - but on the whole they saved those places for the older women. Rachel was there now, rubbing the collar of Caleb's tunic with great aggression; from a quick glance it looked as if she were trying to throttle and drown him at the same time.

Tammie stood up and stretched. The sunshine had pressed down like a great weight on her back as she leaned over, so coming upright made her go dizzy. She'd been working in the sun for about ten minutes and her head felt about to burst. She took off the white cloth covering it to reflect away the sun, and dipped it in the water to cool herself down. Dibs, who was working next to her, stood up as well with a big yawn and a grin. She didn't seem bothered by the sun, and indeed it wasn't that strong yet.

"You're quiet," commented Dibs, casually throwing a little shirt of Jake's towards her mother's pile of clothes on the bank. It missed. "Oh, bum," said Dibs, without looking the least bit concerned.

"Dibs!" came the voice of her mother from further downstream.

Dibs sighed philosophically and waded to the side, where she collected up all the various bits of clothing scattered with great abandonment around the target. Having dunked them in the water to get rid of the flecks of grass and random insects, she wrung them out, placed them a little more carefully on the pile and splashed back to the middle to rejoin Tammie.

"What's up?" she asked. Tammie was no further on at all with the bed sheet she had been working on; she was staring at it thoughtfully, and giving it the occasional half-hearted rub. "Here, I'll help. They aren't half heavy when they're wet."

Dibs grabbed the other end of it, and they carried on together. She normally fooled around quite a bit in the water. It was nothing terribly unusual to discover wet pants down the back of your neck, or find yourself toppling into the water for no apparent reason, if you happened to be standing near her. Even adults were in danger if she thought up something that would look like a genuine accident. Today though, she was being less wild than usual as she sensed Tammie wasn't really in the mood.

"I've got a headache," said Tammie, as they finished the sheet. "I think I'll go for a rest. Coming?"

"No, I'm fine. The sooner it's all done, the sooner we can escape to play!"

How on earth she could think of games after a day's work like this, Tammie didn't know. Dibs was definitely not a Hide and Seek person. Her favourites involved lots of running around and shouting, with a bit of assault thrown in.

Tammie flopped down next to Rachel and massaged her feet. Rachel looked at her suspiciously.

"You been too long in the sun?" she asked.

"No, I don't think so. Very little time at all, really."

"Well, just you make sure you don't."

Tammie lay on her back and watched the blue sky through the moving branches of the trees. It was quiet and peaceful with the birds singing, the women's murmur gentle on her ear, and every now and then a piece of clothing sailing high across her line of vision as part of the Dibs Theory of Effortless Laundry. As Tammie dangled her hand in the water she began to feel much better, and after a while carried on her work.

They broke for lunch at noon to avoid the sun at its hottest, and sat around eating the food they had brought. Tammie lay down again when she had finished, and put her head in her mother's lap. Her headache had nearly gone, but noises seemed louder than usual and the little children's play was disturbing her. They were throwing around a piece of cloth tied into a ball, and toppling over in their efforts to catch it. Normally Tammie would have thrown it for them, but now their movements seemed to irritate her head. When the ball landed near her, it made her jump.

After a few moments she drifted into a snooze, then when she awoke carried on with the washing again. But it didn't last for long before the headache came back worse than ever. The sun on her head felt as if it were striking her, and the glare from the water and the white linen seared her eyes and made them run. She moved back into the shade, although she had only been in the sun a few moments. It seemed to make no difference, and the heat was just as stifling. She felt she couldn't breathe, and her legs went all wobbly. She straightened up and wiped the sweat from her forehead, trying to swallow. Everything seemed to go dark. Her heartbeat was weird, and before she knew what was happening, she was falling.

"Deborah, for the last time!" yelled Dibs's mother.
"It wasn't me!" protested Dibs as she ran to Tammie. "She just fell over - I think she's ill."
They lifted Tammie quickly and carried her to dry ground. She felt so strange; she could hear everything that was going on, but when she tried to speak she couldn't think straight or form her words properly. She seemed to have no control over her arms and legs, and all the time there was this tight, clamped feeling in her head.

"I told her not to stay in the sun long," said Rachel, fussing over her and hiding her concern by being cross.
"We didn't," said Dibs, nearly crying. "We've hardly been any time in the sun today, because she had a headache."

"Oh, how would you know," snapped Rachel. "When you get together you go silly, the pair of you. You probably didn't notice how quick the time was going, laughing and giggling, - and now she's gone and got sunstroke."

Naomi stepped in calmly and took charge.

"Don't worry, Dibs; it's nobody's fault. She'll be fine after a little lie down. Why don't you sit here in the shade and talk quietly with her? You've worked hard; I'm sure your mother won't mind. It's horrible to faint. Tammie will probably feel funny the rest of the day."

Everyone was quickly organised. The others went back to the washing, and Naomi sat Dibs down next to Tammie while they made her comfortable. Tammie felt relieved as she heard her mother's voice, so firm and in control. It had been scary at first, but now everything had slipped back into proportion. She had fainted and needed a rest. Her mother would look after her, and Dibs was going to sit with her and make her laugh.

The day passed much more happily after that. People were kind, and she didn't feel embarrassed any more at making such a spectacle of herself. Naomi and Rachel sat with her as much as they could, and after a while she was able to sit up and chat, although they wouldn't let her work anymore.

Then people started packing things up and disappearing home. Caleb and Benjamin came to help carry, so Tammie didn't need to lift anything. They joked that they'd roll her up in one of the bundles to cart her home, but in fact she didn't need carrying. She was feeling such a lot better that she was able to walk all the way, leaning on Naomi's arm.

Everything would be all right now. When the sun went down it would be the start of Shabbat, the Sabbath day, so she would be able to rest all of tomorrow - and by the following day she would be better again.

But she wasn't, of course.

Chapter Six

WHEN NOTHINGNESS SEEMS BEST

Tammie spent the Sabbath in the normal quiet way, but she couldn't enjoy it. Her father was home again and spoke in the Synagogue, and she was able to wear the belt that had been tantalising her all week - but it didn't seem that important, somehow.

Word had got round that she had been taken ill, and lots of people made a fuss of her. She felt as if they were crowding in. Naomi understood, and as soon as possible they slipped off home, leaving Jairus to follow later.

Although she usually loved the chance to relax each week, she felt restless and uncomfortable. No matter where she went, she couldn't settle. The sun was glaring and made her feel ill again, but the shade was too cold and set her shivering. She dreaded the thought of work the next day, and yet she was bored and fidgety with nothing to do. She drove Rachel mad by wandering around listlessly, - not even interested in eating when it came to the meal time. She wished there was a fire in the kitchen so that she could get warm without the burning, blinding heat of the sun, but on Shabbat they always ate cold food so that no one had to cook.

There was a fire the next day though; Rachel had lit it, being the first one up. Tammie crept out of bed in relief that the night was over and went to sit by it. She had hardly slept at all, feeling frozen even with extra blankets. Everyone else seemed to be about their business; they probably thought Tammie had gone off to have her breakfast alone, on the roof or in another of her favourite places. She curled up weakly by the fire and tried to get to sleep.

It was some time before Naomi found her. She was huddled up in her blankets, shuddering and covered with sweat, her mouth dry and her hands clammy and cold as ice. One look at her was enough to tell Naomi that she had a high temperature. Her face was red and hot to the touch, even though her forehead and hair were soaking wet.

"I don't feel very well," she mumbled.

"I know, darling. Don't try to talk. We'll get you back into bed and make you comfier. Stay here a moment while I fetch someone."

Benjamin carried her back to her room and Naomi put her to bed again, tucking lots of blankets around her and wiping her face with a lovely cold cloth. She helped her to drink something which freshened her mouth, but within a few moments it felt hot, dry and cracked again.

After a little while Jairus came in to see her.

"I don't know," he said cheerfully. "What's going on here? We know you don't like doing the laundry, but this is ridiculous! I hope you realise you've given Rachel a great chance to say 'I told you so'. She won't let you forget this in a hurry. There's only one thing Rachel loves more than giving dire warnings, and that's gloating when you ignore her and she turns out to be right."

Tammie was so exhausted she started to cry; she couldn't hold it back any longer.

"Hey, hey... there's no need for that, love," said Jairus, gently wiping away the tears that she was too weak to care about. "You'll soon be fine."

"I won't, I won't," she sobbed. "It's not sunstroke, it's the fever. I went in to see Sarah. I had to, she was

41

ill, and now I've got it too, just like that woman said. I thought God would make it right. I'm never going to get better, and it's all my fault."

Naomi went pale and gripped Jairus's hand, and even he started slightly. He soon recovered and tried to smile.

"And so he will, yes. God will put it right. Of course he will." He seemed to be trying to convince himself as much as anyone. "We will ask him to, won't we? So you went in to see Sarah? Well, that was very kind. That was a nice thing to do. God likes us to be kind, so he's bound to put it right, isn't he?"

He stopped speaking and swallowed hard. It was as if he had run out of things to say, and wasn't sure of the answer to his own question. Naomi smiled now too; still pale, though. Shockingly pale. It was the first time Tammie could remember her parents looking afraid.

"You were very brave to go in," said Naomi, "and we're proud of you. You'll get better. Just rest and let it take its course, and you'll soon be well."

Tammie tried to smile back through her hiccups, but it wasn't as easy to believe as it had been on the banks of the Korazin. It was a new thing to see that her mother and father didn't know what to do. As she watched them sitting by her bed over the coming days they seemed weak, vulnerable. Other people might sometimes get confused or frightened, but Tammie had always seen in her parents supreme confidence and capability. Now they were unable to do anything, and it seemed stranger because they'd always been the ones everyone turned to.

The people of the town started flocking to the house as soon as the news broke that the Rabbi's daughter had the fever. They crowded into the courtyard, or if the gate was barred they filled the street outside. Three of them even crept into the house and peered round her door as if she were an exhibit in a zoo. They didn't show much concern, they just stared eagerly, so they could boast to their friends and describe in detail her present condition. Only the lack of technology two thousand years ago stopped them posting an update, or taking selfies with poor Tammie lying ill in the background.

Rachel caught those snoopers and threw them violently out of the house, and someone always stood guard after that, - but it didn't stop the flock of people hanging around. Tammie could hear them through the window talking to her father or mother, expressing their grief - sometimes even wailing and crying. But after her parents had gone, Tammie would hear those same people gossiping, avidly exchanging news about how bad her fever was, and whether or not she was expected to live.

It wasn't that all the people were so sickening, but the kind ones kept at a distance. One person Tammie would dearly have liked to see was not allowed to come at all - Dibs. Children and old people seemed to be in the greatest danger; Dibs was as tough as last week's toast and never seemed to get ill, but the risk was too much. On Tammie's birthday Dibs's mother brought her to the street corner opposite Tammie's room, and Jairus carried Tammie to the window. The girls waved across the road and tried to smile, but it was very strange and upsetting. Dibs looked so different. She had obviously been crying; her eyes were red and blotchy. It took a lot to make Dibs cry. They didn't speak. Tammie was too weak, and Dibs seemed choked up. So they just kept smiling, and waving occasionally, and wishing they were somewhere else and this wasn't happening. After a while Dibs's mother gently put an arm round her.

"Come on, love. Let's go now."

Dibs pulled away and began to sniff a little, but allowed herself to be led off. She kept looking back at Tammie as she walked. Then she paused as they reached the corner, to give one last wave. Then she disappeared from sight.

The fever continued to increase as the weeks went by, and the crowds showed no signs of decreasing. Politeness had long been abandoned by the family, and Rachel in particular would often drive them away - but they always came back. Once Naomi herself went out in tears and begged to be left in peace, but even that had no effect.

But all this no longer concerned Tammie; she was completely unaware of anything going on around her. Her temperature raged, and she fought day and night against the tightness in her chest that stopped her breathing, and the bedclothes which irritated her hot, hypersensitive skin. It was like being permanently in a nightmare, with weird and frightening images in her mind that never seemed to leave. Time meant nothing anymore, nor did real life; it was as if nothing existed but the clashing jumble of dreams inside her head.

Then one day into this frenzy came a soft, crooning lullaby. The soothing voice was singing, singing, so gently and peacefully; never stopping, but patiently and sweetly singing on. Tammie heard it and began to remember who she was again. It made her think of her childhood, and her mother - no, not her mother; what was it? Yes. Sitting on the lap of an old woman, looking at the boats on the lake. The song made her stop her constant thrashing and rolling from side to side to listen. As she became calmer she found that she was

44

able to open her eyes, and she saw Old Sarah sitting on her bed, stroking her hand and singing to her. She tried to focus her wandering mind to consider this. Sarah was ill - in fact she must surely be dead by now - and so this must be just another picture thrown up by her confused imagination. But what did it matter? At least it was a nice one.

And so things continued; feverish struggling against nightmares and horrors, no rest, no comfort, no consciousness of anyone or anything - and then the beautiful old voice coming stealing back in with psalms and lullabies that would quieten her for a time. Many weeks went by like this, although to Tammie it was as if she had been in this state forever.

Then the nature of the illness changed again, as it passed into its final stages and death drew near. She became weaker and lost the strength to battle against it. The fever had wasted her away and sapped all her energy. She lay motionless, lapsing vaguely in and out of consciousness; unmoving and uncaring, too exhausted even to be unhappy or afraid, too drained to know who she was or what was happening except that it was a relief just to lie there.

And this is how it was for a time, as she drifted further and further away from any awareness. Then finally there was nothing, really.

Nothing at all.

Chapter Seven

THE MAN WITH THE NICE EYES

"Little Girl."

It was funny. Tammie usually hated being called a little girl, but somehow she didn't mind when this voice said it. She hoped he would speak again.

"Little girl, get up!"

She wanted to. She wanted to do what he said, but also to see him, so she opened her eyes and sat up.

The man who had spoken was sitting on her bed, holding her hand and smiling at her. She smiled back and laughed. He seemed ordinary, really: not *that* old for a grown-up - younger than her father, certainly - and dressed much the same as a working man. But he had a nice smile, and nice eyes. His eyes seemed to have the strength and wisdom of her father, and the kindness of her mother - yet somehow, at the same time, there was definitely the mischievous twinkle of Dibs.

She noticed her parents in the room and slipped out of bed to go and hug them. The expressions of utter amazement on their faces struck her as funny, so she laughed again for sheer joy as she put her arms round them and kissed them. They clung to her as if they would never let her go again, and as the shock wore off and the relief sank in, they began to weep and laugh and thank God as they realised that she was here, safe in their arms.

It was all so happy and so perfect that it seemed as if the illness had never really happened. All Tammie could think about was the peace she felt, and the joy and light-heartedness. And stew bubbling in a huge pot. And licking honey straight from the spoon, and the smell of bread as it comes out of the oven, and lemon cakes, and oranges that cover you in stickiness as you slurp the juice out..... She was most certainly feeling better.

"You'd better give her something to eat; she'll be hungry," said the man.

"I'm *starving*!" said Tammie, giving her father a bear hug as if she were going to eat him. She heard a laugh she recognised and swung round to see Rebekah's husband Simon, grinning at her appetite just as when he gave her the lemon cake - however long ago that had been. Daniel's two big brothers were there as well: James and John, fishermen, and partners of Simon. It was quite a party. Just who this strange man with the nice eyes was (and what they were all doing in her bedroom) was not at all clear - but who cared?

After all the crying and laughing had settled down a bit, Jairus pulled himself together enough to attempt an introduction. The man's name was Jesus, apparently, and he had come to stay in Capernaum since Tammie got ill. He was obviously a friend of the three fishermen, but Tammie guessed he wasn't one himself, as his home town was Nazareth. That was some way to the west in the more mountainous regions, quite far from the lake.

"Let's go outside and get madam here something to eat," said Naomi, as she ushered them through. "You will join us for supper?"

They broke rowdily into the hushed atmosphere of the courtyard like a wave hitting a beach. Caleb was sitting gazing at the floor, holding a huge hanky limp in his hands; Benjamin leant against the gatepost with tears flowing quietly and endlessly down his face; Rachel and

Old Sarah were seated, praying together, on the steps - Rachel sobbing uncontrollably. The looks on their faces as they saw Tammie spring into their midst were a picture, and the whole process of laughing and crying and hugging had to be done all over again. But Old Sarah simply rose to her feet and smiled at Jesus, with a beautiful glow of pride and love. She looked as if this was exactly what she had been expecting, but that didn't make her joy any the less.

"Who would have thought it! Who *would* have thought it!" Rachel kept gasping, as if she just had to say something, and could think of nothing else. Nobody could remember having seen her so emotional; she took delight in being annoyingly unflappable, whatever the circumstances.

"And here you are, the fever all cleared up - who would have said it was possible? Well! And we went and distressed you for no reason," she continued breathlessly to Jairus. "I am so sorry. We would never have sent word to tell you she was dead if we'd realised." She stroked Tammie's hair and gazed at her in wonder. "But she did seem dead, you know. I've seen a few people when they've passed over - my old mother, for one - and I was as sure as possible this child had gone."

"She'd gone, all right," said Sarah quietly. "I've seen a good few more than you."

Tammie listened to this in surprise, then thought of something much more important.

"Well I'm not dead now, and I'm hungry. It's essential I get something to eat; this Jesus person said so."

"Oh did he now?" said Rachel, recovering her old self a little and bustling off to the kitchen. "He hasn't been looking after invalids and mourning lost children for goodness knows how long. We shall have to see if we've got anything in the larder. I don't know, - kids! They worry you sick getting fevers, then they go and die, and all of a sudden they bob up and expect to be fed as if you've had nothing else to do...."

"Let's go and spread the news!" said Benjamin to Caleb, barely able to stand still. "Everyone thinks she's dead - just wait till we tell them!"

"No," said Jesus, and they stopped in their tracks. "Don't tell anyone what's happened here."

Caleb raised his eyebrows and whistled through his teeth.

"That ain't going to be so easy," he said. "This entire town, and more, knew how sick she was - and they must all have heard by now that she died. Unless we lock her in her room the rest of her life, they're going to notice she's alive."

"Let them notice by all means. If they want, they can work it out for themselves."

Caleb laughed. "Oh, I see. Let the deed speak for itself? That won't please 'em. They like to know everything that goes on."

"We can't tell them what happened anyway," said Benjamin. "We don't know ourselves."

"You heard the man; work it out," retorted Caleb with a chuckle, and Benjamin sighed and shook his head as if it were beyond him.

Tammie had now had chance to take in the fact that Sarah was looking as tall and strong as she used to; a beautiful old woman again. Huh? I mean - it was great, of course, but… huh? She went to Sarah, puzzled, and took her hands.

"When I was ill I kept thinking you were by my bed, comforting me."

"I was, child," said Sarah.

"I thought you must have died by now. What happened; why didn't you?"

Sarah laughed and nodded towards Jesus. "My healing came from the same place as yours. Not so surprising, since it was the same fever, is it?"

"As you told me, Sarah, more than once," said Jairus. "Your counsel was wise. I wish I'd followed it sooner." He gave a little bow to Jesus. "I should have asked you to come to my daughter weeks ago, sir," he said. "I even pleaded with you to heal the centurion's servant - not one of our own people - yet I was afraid to ask this. It was good of you to come, when you knew how long I'd been holding back."

"No harm done," said Jesus. "The glory to God will be all the greater. Don't be afraid anymore."

Jairus offered Jesus and his friends seats in a corner of the courtyard and they sat together, deep in conversation. Tammie noticed the respectful way her father spoke to the stranger, and listened eagerly to all his replies. He must be someone very learned and important. She asked her mother what he was.

"Jesus is a carpenter, darling," said Naomi.

A carpenter? He didn't seem much like any carpenter Tammie had ever known, and Jairus didn't look about to put in an order for a new table.

"Does Daddy know he's a carpenter?" she asked, wondering if there had been some misunderstanding.

"Oh yes," said Naomi, then hesitated. "I suppose he isn't a carpenter at the moment, but that is where, well... his skill - or rather, his training is. It's a bit tricky to explain."

Tammie started to devour her first proper meal since what seemed like years ago, and to enjoy taking pleasure in food again. She watched her father as she ate, deep in conversation. This was another new side to him - one that she had rarely, if ever, seen before. The desperate, confused man had gone. But so had the other Jairus: the respected, confident teacher who* knew everything. He seemed like a student, almost; eager to learn. They reminded Tammie of the times she had seen Daniel sitting by her father, still asking questions long after the class had finished - but it was Jairus who looked like Daniel, and Jesus seemed like the Rabbi.

Jairus wasn't the only one to have changed. Simon had blossomed, - if blossomed is the right word to use about a hulking great fisherman. He was at ease to the point of being positively chatty; not a shred of awkwardness remained. If anything, he may have gone too far the other way. Being friends with this carpenter seemed to have quite an effect on people. Even Simon's name had changed. Naomi explained that Jesus had given him a nickname - 'Peter', which meant 'the rock'. This Jesus must be a pretty good judge of character, Tammie thought with a grin.

John didn't seem too different. Tammie liked John. He was less than ten years older than her, and though he was grown up now, Tammie could remember when she was little and he used to play with the others on the wasteland. She and Daniel would get him to swing them round, and he never said no. He was always kind and good fun. If anything, he was now *more* boyish and bubbling over than before Jesus had come on the scene.

A lot of things had obviously been going on. They deserved her fullest investigation, but for the time being she was happy giving all her consideration to the food.

Chapter Eight

IN THE COOL OF THE EVENING

The first thing that struck Tammie when she finally emerged from her plate was that there was no one around but themselves; in all the excitement she hadn't even noticed. The last she had known, the whole place had been swarming with neighbours hot on the trail of juicy gossip - as persistent as wasps, and about as welcome. She turned to Rachel in surprise.

"Where did everybody go?"

Rachel grinned.

"It was him," she said, nodding towards Jesus. "I've never seen people scamper off so quick. He looks quiet, but he's got a tongue in him. If he gives you a look or a firm word, you don't feel inclined to go against him! I don't think the good folks who were hanging round here had quite got the measure of him."

Tammie liked the thought of this man with nice eyes putting to flight the people who had made her mother cry. She hugged herself in anticipation. Rachel was unable to stop a smirk of satisfaction creeping across her face.

"The crowds had got a bit less. They got distracted by this Jesus, and were following him round like a travelling show. But as you got so's you were about to die - and he'd gone away cross the lake anyway - they were back, worse than ever. Then when you died - well, they set up wailing and keening, you know how they do, and they burst in here; we couldn't give your poor mother any privacy. They just would *not* shift. And then Jesus came, with your dad. He sorted them."

"Why did Jesus come?" asked Tammie.

"His boat had been sighted," said Rachel, "and your

52

dad had hurried to ask him to do for you what he did for Sarah. But then you passed on, so Caleb and Benjamin went to break the news and stop Jesus coming. We didn't want to waste his time. He's in great demand, you know; people traipsing miles to be healed, or whatever they call it. We didn't think there was any point him coming, now you were dead. But he came anyway - I don't know why."

"He came to perform an even greater miracle than the one he'd been asked for," said Sarah.

"When he came in through the gate," said Naomi, anxious to join in, "he told us not to be afraid, just to believe. I wasn't sure what he meant, but he was so calm and certain I somehow felt it was all in his hands. You feel you can trust him, don't you?"

Sarah nodded.

"Anyhow," continued Rachel, not to be robbed of telling the best bit, "he walks into the courtyard and looks around at all the so-called mourners making their racket, and you could tell he was angry. He said you weren't dead but asleep. I don't know if he meant it literally or - or metaphysically..."

"Metaphorically," corrected Naomi gently.

"Yes, well, when they heard this, they showed themselves for the hypocrites they are. One minute they'd been weeping, but now they all started jeering and mocking him. Fine way to behave in a house that's in mourning. Well, he simply turns and looks at them, then he puts them out of the house, just like that! He didn't shout - he barely said anything, just told them to get out. I don't know how he did it, but they melted away like snow. They won't be back again in a hurry! It's good to remember; I was too upset at the time to enjoy it."

Jesus came over to see Tammie.

"How do you feel now?" he asked.

"Wicked!" said Tammie. "I'd like to go for a walk; I've been cooped up for so long." An idea occurred to her. "Would you like to come? I could show you the places Daddy and I go, and we could have a nice talk."

Jesus laughed. "You had better ask your parents. They may not be happy with their daughter going off with a stranger."

"If it wasn't for you, sir, we wouldn't have a daughter," said Jairus.

"Darling, Jesus may be tired, or have important things to do," said Naomi to Tammie.

"A walk before supper would be very nice," said Jesus.

"Come on, then!" cried Tammie, grabbing his hand and dragging him through the gate. "We won't be too long," she shouted over her shoulder, and they were off.

Tammie knew exactly where she wanted to take him. The olive groves that started just beyond her house were cool and shady, and except at harvest you would rarely see anyone there. They did come across a farmer tending the trees, but he didn't seem inclined to bother them. In fact he dropped his spade and stared at Tammie till his eyes nearly burst from his head like spring-loaded ping pong balls. Then he turned and scuttled off in a combination of fear and excitement he could barely contain. The news was on its way to the town, but Jesus and Tammie didn't care either way about that.

They strolled along very happily, and chatted as if they had known each other for ages. Tammie was doing most of the talking, it has to be said, but Jesus didn't seem annoyed by this. Tammie noticed that he was one of those people who takes a genuine interest in what you have to say.

She wanted to know a bit more about him, so she asked whether he was living in Capernaum permanently.

"No," he said. "I travel around Galilee, and sometimes further. But I often come back here, so you'll see me quite a bit."

"Ah, I understand," said Tammie, nodding her head very wisely. "You're one of those Intin... Itrin... Ite... Wandering Preachers."

"Itinerants; yes, I suppose you could call me that. I don't think that's the word your father's friends use, though."

"Don't they like you?"

"No."

He didn't seem too upset, he just stated it as a fact.

"I like you," said Tammie.

"Good," he said. "I like you too, so that's settled."

"Will you call me Tammie, then? All my friends do." Her father had introduced her as Tamar.

Jesus laughed. "You don't like your name?"

"Yuk," was Tammie's definite opinion. "Mind you," she added brightening, "there are a couple of Tamars in the Holy Writings."

"That's true," he said. "One of them was an ancestor of mine." In the Temple at Jerusalem there were family trees for everyone, going right the way back. It gave reading the scrolls an extra zing if you kept an eye out to see if one of your relatives would pop up.

"She hated her name when she was your age too," Jesus added.

It didn't occur to Tammie till years later to wonder how he knew that, and by the time it did, she felt she knew the answer anyway. But just now she was too bothered about her name.

"It's so lame," she complained. "It means 'Palm Tree'. So many names have such lovely meanings, and I get stuck with 'Palm Tree'."

"I don't know," said Jesus, "I'm very fond of trees."

"But not to be called after one!"

"The palm is a sign of Victory. And palm trees are tall and graceful; the name Tamar given to a woman in the old days meant that she was very beautiful."

"Really?" said Tammie in surprise. "But I'm not beautiful."

"You'll grow out of that," said Jesus, teasing her.

"I don't think I even want to be beautiful," she said, after some consideration.

"You'll probably grow out of that too."

"My other names are even worse: Bilkiah and Keren Happuch. I don't know what they mean, but it's probably something ghastly."

"Keren Happuch is 'Splendour of bright colours' - another indication of beauty. And Bilkiah means 'Revival'... 'Coming back to life'. After today, I don't think you could have a better name."

Tammie listened to this wide-eyed, and began to wonder if perhaps her names were pretty good after all.

"Well, that's very interesting," she said. "My parents' names are nice. Naomi means 'Pleasantness', and Jairus is 'He will enlighten'. That's a great name for someone who spends all his time teaching people about God."

"A very good name," said Jesus.

"Yours is short for Jehoshua, isn't it? What does that stand for?"

"'The Salvation of the Lord'," said Jesus.

"That's nice," said Tammie.

It was so lovely to be out walking in the warm breezes and the fresh smells of trees and flowers. Tammie breathed in deeply and thought how beautiful everything was.

"This is just like it was in the beginning," she said. "Adam and Eve used to walk with God in the Garden of Eden, in the cool of the evening."

"Yes, I know," said Jesus.

"And then everything went wrong," she continued, "and evil got invited in. And now we can't walk with God or be close to him, because he's too pure and glorious. Did you know that in the Temple at Jerusalem, where the presence of God lives, there is a sort of curtain thing to separate even the priests from God? My daddy told me."

"Right," said Jesus. "It separates the Holy Place from the Most Holy Place."

"Even the priests have to be protected from the sight of God," she said, shaking her head sadly. "I so much want to get close to him, don't you? But there always has to be a barrier. That veil curtain thing is precious; it's very old, and it's supposed to be really beautiful, but it's there to keep us from God. This is probably a terrible thing to say, but sometimes I want to march straight in there and rip that curtain in half."

"Me too," said Jesus.

Chapter Nine

THE LAW TURNED ON ITS HEAD

They met Simon Peter and the other two resting at the edge of the grove as they made their way back, so Jesus stopped off to talk with them. Tammie continued home, promising to call them when supper was served.

As she went in through the gates she saw the very last person she would have expected to see inside their house, or anyone's house. There was Salome, sitting arm in arm with Tammie's mother. 'Huh?' times a thousand! Tammie stopped short and gaped in astonishment. As soon as Salome saw her she rushed forward and embraced her, gasping "Oh my dear, I haven't been able to hold you in my arms since you were a little baby!"

Tammie just gazed at her; happy but totally bemused.

"I don't know why you are looking at me so surprised," smiled Salome. "I have just as much right to be astounded at you. Last night I heard you were at death's door."

"I'm afraid I can't tell you what happened," said Tammie.

"Oh, you don't need to," said Salome. "Jesus was here - that's enough to explain anything. But I can tell you what happened to me; it's no secret, half the town saw it!"

"I could have told you about Salome myself," said Jairus, "I was there too - but with everything else.... "

"It slipped your mind!" laughed Salome.

They all sat down again, and Salome continued telling them what had happened.

"I had been plucking up courage to speak to Jesus since he first came here - right from the time when he healed Sarah, and restored Jethro's hand in the Synagogue. Do you remember?"

"Did he put Jethro's hand right?" butted in Tammie. Jethro's hand had been withered from childhood; he couldn't use it at all.

"Yes, in front of everyone," said Naomi. "It's good as new. Now hush, let's listen."

"But I was afraid," continued Salome. "For one thing, he always has such a crowd round him, and I felt embarrassed to speak in front of so many. And also - well, it's in the past now - but I knew you didn't approve of him, Rabbi. There's been such a lot of talk about whether he's a blasphemer, or worse, and I wanted to be sure. And the people he mixes with - the rumours you hear - and the way he invited Matthew to be one of his closest followers... "

"Matthew the... the Tax Collector?" asked Tammie, open-mouthed in astonishment. She had nearly called him Matthew the Something Else, she was so used to the variety of rude names the people of Capernaum had made up for him. "Matthew the Levite? That Matthew?"

"Oh yes," said Rachel, who had not been above inventing a few choice names to throw at him whenever she passed his booth. "He's a follower of Jesus, and has given shedloads of money back to people, and Jesus says we must be nice to him."

"Well!" said Tammie, as if that were even more amazing than the business with Jethro's hand.

"So you see, I didn't know what to think about Jesus," continued Salome, when she could get a word in. "I would never go to anyone I thought might be against God. So I watched him, and I came to the conclusion I think you have now, too." Jairus nodded and smiled, slightly ashamed. "I was sure he was from God, but there were still all the crowds, and that fear of drawing attention to myself. But while he was away this last time, I made myself promise that when he came back I would do it."

"How could you be sure he would come back again?" asked Tammie.

"I needed him," Salome said, very simply. "I can't explain it, but I knew he would come back. So I had it all planned. I wasn't going to say anything, just mix in with the crowd. It was a bit daunting to go in amongst those jostling people - you know how weak I am. Was, I mean. But I would push my way to the front, then reach out and touch his cloak. I knew that would be enough to heal me, and I wouldn't need to disturb him at all."

"Your faith is wonderful," said Jairus. "It's a real lesson to me. It reminds me of Marcellus, the centurion, when he sent me to ask Jesus to heal his servant of the fever. Marcellus said he wasn't worthy to have Jesus in his house, so he was happy for Jesus just to command a healing."

"And it was done for him, just as he believed," said Sarah. "Lucius was healed, - and so were you, Salome."

"Yes, but it wasn't quite as I had expected," laughed Salome.

"What happened?" asked Naomi.

"Everything went perfectly. I touched his cloak, and I felt such a sense of well-being I couldn't describe. It was strange," she added, thinking it over. "It was as if the Law suddenly started working backwards; everything was turned on its head. Usually if I touch anyone, they become unclean like me. But when I touched him... well, I took on his cleanness - that's the only way I can describe it. I really thought I had got away with it, but he stopped dead and asked who had touched him."

"It seemed a ridiculous question," explained Jairus. "There was an enormous crowd; I had only just managed to fight through myself, to ask him to come to Tammie. We all wondered how he could possibly ask who had touched him - we were being crushed! But of course, he knew something special had happened."

"I was terrified," went on Salome. "I thought he would be angry, and I felt ashamed to confess it was me - but he was so kind." Her face suddenly clouded over, as she remembered what happened next. "It was then that your men arrived to say Tammie was dead."

"I actually hated you at that point, Salome," admitted Jairus. "I felt as if you had taken - stolen - the healing that would have been for Tammie, if only we had carried on to my house. But things don't seem to work like that with Jesus. He told me to trust, and I did somehow. After all that time of suspecting him, I had reached the point where there was nothing else to do."

"I wonder who he is?" pondered Benjamin. "He's related to that John who went round baptising people in the Jordan - that one you had meetings about on the trip to Jerusalem, Rabbi. John got quite a following round here; some said he was a prophet of God, till he got arrested. Simon and Andrew seemed to think he was, certainly. Do you suppose this Jesus could be a prophet too? What do you suppose he is?"

"Hungry," said Rachel, having recovered her ability to be down-to-earth in the face of all heavenly considerations. "We're supposed to be feeding him, and I think it's the least we can do."

The meal was quickly served, and Jesus and his friends were called. As they were about to start everyone hesitated and looked at Jairus; he would normally give thanks to God, but he seemed almost shy, as if he didn't feel it was up to him. He turned to Jesus.

"Would you...?" he asked hesitantly, and Jesus smiled and thanked God for the food, and all the other blessings he had given them that day.

Tammie attacked her food with great relish, and Simon Peter laughed at her once more.

"Eating again?" he asked. "You only had a full meal a couple of hours ago!"

Tammie considered this carefully. "But you see, I hadn't eaten anything for weeks and weeks," she explained. "There's still an awful lot of room to fill up."

Everyone laughed.

"I'm serious!" she protested indignantly with her mouth full.

"We know, darling," said Naomi. "That's why we're laughing."

Tammie shook her head and gave up trying to make them understand. There was something in the process of growing up that seemed to make a person incapable of having a really good attitude to food.

They hadn't been eating long when they heard footsteps running up to the gate. They paused in their meal, expecting a knock, but the footsteps just stopped abruptly and there was silence.

"Perhaps you would see who it is?" said Jairus to Jesus. "It may be that the people are beginning to gather again."

Jesus went to the gate and opened it, and Tammie could just see through it a very familiar figure.

"Who are you?" said Jesus.

"Dibs,.. I mean Diborah, no, Deborah," said Dibs, gazing at him nervously. She remained like that for a moment, then suddenly dropped a little curtsy.

"Pleased to meet you," said Jesus. He beckoned her in. "Tammie, there's a Dibs here. I presume it belongs with you?"

Dibs edged in cautiously past him, watching him all the time as if she were scared he might perform a miracle if she took her eyes off him. When she was safely inside she looked around at the assembled company.

"Hello," she said to Tammie after a pause, then, as if this was the reason she had come, "I've got your birthday present. Mum wouldn't let me give it on the day in case it upset you."

Naomi fetched some supper for her, and she and Tammie sat together on one of the couches that had been carried out from the dining room in honour of their guest.

"Everything has been so exciting I'd forgotten I had a birthday when I was ill," said Tammie. "So I'm twelve now. Two years older than you again."

"I'll catch up," said Dibs, shovelling a steady succession of food into her mouth. No one could accuse Dibs of not having a positive attitude towards food.

"Not completely, you won't," said Tammie. "I'll always be at least a year ahead. It's funny though; it looked as if you would be able to overtake me. I wasn't going to go past twelve."

"Don't say that," said Dibs, stopping and looking unhappily at Tammie.

"But it didn't happen," said Tammie. "It can't hurt us."

"Yay!" said Dibs, loud again.

They ploughed on with their food, but Dibs kept an

eye on Jesus all the same; she didn't quite trust him, it seemed. Tammie looked around at everyone too. This was the best time of her life she could ever remember - better than any birthday or feast day. Happy, full of life and health, surrounded by nearly everyone she most loved in the world. She felt as if everything was just beginning, as if this were the very first of all the good times.

When the plates had been cleared, no one seemed inclined to go home, so they sat around talking. Sarah was humming a psalm in the corner, and one or two others picked up the tune and joined in. Soon they were all singing in that sleepy, peaceful way you only get when sitting under a clear night sky, with a warm, gentle breeze, good company and a full stomach. Tammie felt as if she was going to burst. She wanted it never to end.

But eventually people started dispersing, and there were leave-takings and see-you-in-the-mornings all round. James and John promised to call at Dibs's house to let them know Dibs was staying over, and the household was left alone.

Dibs and Tammie got ready for bed and settled down, still talking long after they had snuffed out the lamp. Tammie was telling Dibs all about her new friend Jesus, but Dibs didn't seem convinced.

"They're saying bad things about him."

"Who are?"

"They."

"Is anyone saying good things about him?"

"Oh yes, lots of people are saying good things."

"Well then," said Tammie, happy at having proved her point.

"He scares me," said Dibs, after a moment thinking about this.

"Why?"

"I don't know. I don't understand him, and I don't know what he's going to do next."

"That's because you don't know him yet."

"Oh."

"And people who are unpredictable are more fun. You're unpredictable."

"Am I?" said Dibs, brightening. She liked the idea of being unpredictable. "Your birthday present is unpredickable. You'll like it. I'll show it you tomorrow."

She turned over, and thought some more.

"My dad says he's a - a vandal and a home wrecker," she said after a few minutes.

"Who?" asked Tammie, who had nearly dropped off to sleep.

"Jesus," said Dibs.

"Jesus?" said Tammie. "Why on earth would anyone call him that?"

"You haven't seen our roof," said Dibs.

Chapter Ten

DIBS'S ROOF

Dibs was annoyingly difficult to wake the next morning. She could sleep through anything, which is no bad thing if you have to share a room with thousands of little brothers and sisters. Tammie lay there for a while, idly flicking bits of roasted grain at her. She was aiming to get them into Dibs's open mouth, but she was a lousy shot and they weren't waking Dibs anyway, so it seemed a much better idea to eat the grain herself, and tickle Dibs's nose with a piece of straw. That had no effect either, in spite of a few monumental sneezes. Tammie seriously considered a bucket of water, but it seemed foolish to play a joke on someone that would leave your own bed sopping wet, so she settled for pulling the sheet from under her.

Dibs crashed to the floor and rolled to the other side of the room, then sat up and looked at Tammie.

"You've probably squashed your present now," she said. "Don't blame me."

And then she lay down and went straight back to sleep.

"Oh no you don't!" laughed Tammie, pinning her down and tickling her until there seemed no further danger.

"Where's this present, then?" she asked impatiently as they went out to the courtyard.

Dibs smiled importantly and started fiddling around in the fold of her belt, where there was a large and intriguing lump.

"Here it is," she said. "My brother Joel found it, and I got it off him by promising not to tell Dad who it

66

was who used his hat as a water carrier. I've been looking after it for you. It's the biggest one Joel's ever seen."

A simply ginormous toad emerged with difficulty from Dibs's clothing, and gazed solemnly at Tammie, who gazed back at it in the same wide-eyed, unblinking way.

"Isn't it brilliant?" said Dibs proudly. "I knew you'd like it."

"It's... absolutely amazing," said Tammie, perfectly truthfully. "I had no idea they could grow so big. Thank you very much indeed. It will be very... interesting to watch and look after. Very educational."

"Oh yes, very educational. And very useful, too. You can slip it into people's dinners, or down their necks, or all sorts of things."

Naomi had come over to see the present, and was now staring eye to eye with the toad, open-mouthed, in much the same way as Tammie.

"They make very good pets," said Dibs. Naomi seemed unconvinced. "You can talk to them," Dibs added, by way of further explanation.

"Well, yes, I suppose you can," admitted Naomi.

"My brother has several at home."

"Has he," was Naomi's only comment on that. "Well, we'll have to find a very... special place to keep it. Somewhere nice and far from the house, so that he won't feel too crowded. Is it a he?"

"I'm not sure. It's hard to tell," said Dibs, who was obviously seeing herself as a great authority on toads these days. "We could try and find out... "

"No, no - let's leave it its privacy," said Naomi hastily.

"It might be important in deciding its name,

though," said Dibs, having a good look.

"I'm sure it won't mind what name we give it. Just leave it please, Dibs," said Naomi, edging away, then remembering something very important she had to do in the kitchen.

"Oh, I do love you, Dibs," said Tammie, wiping the tears from her eyes as she tried to stop laughing.

"I am unpredickable, aren't I?" said Dibs happily.

They found a large box as a temporary home for Hezekiah the Toad, and left him exploring his new environment. He seemed content with it - but wouldn't you be, if you had just spent the night in Dibs's belt? Then Tammie went round to Dibs's house to say hello, and to see what had been going on.

Quite a lot, it would appear. A large chunk had gone from the roof of the main room, and I do mean *large*. This hole was about seven feet long! Tammie stared at it in wonderment.

"Did Jesus do *that*?" she asked.

"Well no, he didn't exactly do it himself," said Dibs, "but my dad blames him for it anyway. He won't be invited back again, that's for sure."

Work was underway on the repairs. Five men Tammie didn't know were busy climbing up and down ladders, carrying materials, hammering and so on. They were working very hard, and singing away and joking to each other equally hard, and praising God. Dibs's father, Tobias, was just standing looking up at them with a gloomy expression, shaking his head from time to time.

"What on earth happened?" asked Tammie.

"Dad wanted to know a bit about this Jesus," said

Dibs. "My uncle Thomas is really keen; he's become one of his followers, and we were hearing all sorts from him. So Dad asked Jesus round."

"Well, that sounds fairly normal. You don't usually ask someone to tea and end up with a courtyard instead of a living room."

"No," said Dibs, "but if you invite Jesus to tea, you get everyone from Capernaum and Korazin and Bethsaida and Chinnereth and Magdala as well."

"All of them?"

"A lot of them."

"You'd run out of cups."

"We ran out of floor, too. They filled the room, and Mum opened the big doors so that people could sit in the street and still hear Jesus. And he was talking to them, and telling stories and stuff, and my dad was looking proud that he'd got your dad and all these other Rabbis in his house. I was at the side of the crowd. Dad wouldn't let me in the house, he said that was for important people. I think he thought I might show him up."

"No. Really?"

"You can shut your face," said Dibs, thumping her. "Then, as Jesus was going on and on, we began to notice bits of dust falling. Just a very little at first, then straw, and even a few tiles. We looked up, and we could see daylight! I'm not kidding. There was this hole, getting bigger all the time. Dad was going mad, but he was trying to stay polite 'cos of his guests. I was nearly wetting myself, it was so funny. The Rabbis were being all dignified, but they'd got this dried mud on their posh robes. You should have seen your dad, it looked like terminal dandruff. Jesus just sat there, looking up, and waited. Then when it was *really* huge it all went dark for a moment, and this mat thing started coming through, - with these two hands clinging tight to the edge, and these scared little eyes sort of peeping over. The look on my dad's face was hysterical. The mat was lowered right the way down by some men on the roof; it landed bang in front of Jesus, and there was this paralysed bloke lying on it. It would be great to do as a party trick. I wish I'd thought of it."

"Why didn't they just carry him in?" asked Tammie.

"They couldn't have - there was so many people you couldn't get near. They must've gone round the back and up the steps. They'd carried him for miles; I s'pose they weren't going to lug him all the way back without seeing Jesus."

"So then Jesus healed the man?" said Tammie.

"Well, no. It was a real let-down. He just smiled at him and said his sins were forgiven."

"I suppose that's more important," said Tammie. "Jesus knows what he's doing."

"Yeah, - but I bet the man's friends were narked they'd have to cart him home again! Anyhow, then Jesus turned to your dad and them, and asked why they were thinking bad things about him. They didn't look too pleased at that. He said they were thinking he was doing blasphemy because only God can forgive sins, or something. That word 'Blasphemy' is dead good, isn't it? I like that joke, 'Blasphemy! Blasphemy! Everyone's got it bl… ' No, that's not right."

"That's 'Infamy', you numptie."

"Oh yeah. Well then Jesus asked them which was easiest, forgive the man's sins or make him walk. He didn't bother to wait for an answer, he just turned to the man, told him to pick his mat up and go home, and he did!"

"Well, of course he did," said Tammie proudly. "I can just imagine the man now; at home, celebrating with his family."

"No, that's him there," said Dibs, pointing to the most energetic, most lively, most leapingest-around of all the workmen.

"Oh, *wow!*" said Tammie, staring at him in amazement as he shinned quickly up a ladder with a load of tiles, then jumped down from the top rung and ran off to get another lot.

Of course that was not what Tammie actually said, as it is very modern, and Tammie was speaking Aramaic anyway - but what she said was an expression of such surprise, pleasure and general flabbergastidity, it can only adequately be translated as 'Oh, *wow!*'

"He came back with the friends who carried him," said Dibs, "and insisted on giving my dad some gifts for the bother, and repairing the roof too. They reckon they're going to make it better than it was before, ready for when the rains start again."

Dibs's uncle Thomas came out of the house and stood by his brother. They were twins, and it was always funny to watch them because the likeness carried much further than just their appearance. They had the same opinions, facial expressions, mannerisms, everything. Dibs and Joel would often try to confuse the townspeople by sending them to the wrong person. If Thomas and Tobias had been the sort of men who liked a joke, they could have had endless scope for amusement. But joking, along with scuba diving and Scottish country dancing, was a means of spending time and energy that would simply never have crossed their minds.

They stood together now, rubbing their chins and looking up dismally as the work progressed apace, rather like the crowd that gathers when you are attempting to change a wheel; all shaking their heads and pointing out that you are doing it wrong, but never offering to help you get it right.

"Not enough straw, you see," Tammie heard Tobias say as she and Dibs slipped away.

"Got to have straw. Never get the consistency right without straw," agreed Thomas.

"That's what I told them. 'It's your consistency,' I said. 'You got to have your consistency.'"

Thomas shook his head and whistled through his teeth to express his misgivings. "It'll be the rains very soon," he said. "Reckon we shall see then."

"Reckon we shall."

If Jesus had chosen Thomas as one of his closest followers, thought Tammie, then *he* had a pretty good sense of humour, that was for certain.

Chapter Eleven

BLESSED ARE THE PERCIVALS

There was one friend Tammie still hadn't caught up with since bouncing back out of the grave, so to speak, so she headed to the lake. Daniel wasn't there, but his father Zebedee steered her right; he said that recently, when work was finished, Daniel had been spending a lot of time on the banks of the Korazin.

Tammie followed the stream upwards until she got to the trees where they did the washing, and then she heard a voice she knew well - though she didn't recognise the tone, or the authority. Daniel sounded like an experienced preacher. Something about loving your enemies? Something about storing up treasure in heaven, so your heart would be there too. Tammie crept a little closer to watch from behind a tree.

"Do not worry about your life - what you will eat or drink, or what you will wear. Look at the birds of the air!" Daniel did a big gesture, as if there were birds like a large hat in an arc right over his head. "They don't grow food, and yet your heavenly Father feeds them. Aren't you much more valuable than them? Of course you are, it's a no-brainer. And can you add even a minute to your life by worrying?"

Daniel stopped abruptly and fished a tatty scroll from his belt. After a quick consultation he carried on as if nothing had happened.

"And can you add even an hour to your life by worrying? Look at the flowers of the field!" Another wide gesture, across the ground this time - though all Tammie could see was grass. "If God dresses them so beautifully, he's not going to forget about you. Your

Father in heaven knows you need food and clothes and that, so chill. Seek first his Kingdom and righteousness, and the other stuff will be given you as well."

Daniel seemed satisfied with that. He stopped and consulted his scroll to pick a bit to do next. Who was he talking to? The field was deserted apart from the birds and flowers he was on about, and they didn't seem to be taking much notice. He was off again.

"Ask and it will be given to you. Seek and you will find. Knock and the door will be opened to you. If your son asks you for bread, will you give him a slice of rock? Or if he asks for fish, will you give him a live snake? And you're rubbish parents, compared to God. So just think - if even you can give your kids nice stuff, how much more will your heavenly Father give good gifts, if you ask him!"

Tammie came out of hiding and drew closer to listen properly. Daniel threw her a grin, but carried on declaiming to the empty meadow. He was on a roll, and nothing was going to stop his big finish.

"Treat other people the way you would like them to treat you. Because that's everything the Holy Writings have been saying. That's the whole of the Law and the Prophets, right there."

Tammie burst into applause and Daniel tucked the scroll away, coming over to see her.

"You're alive," he said - pleased, but remarkably un-astounded. "Good. I knew you would be, once I heard your father had gone to Jesus."

"Aren't you even a teeny bit surprised?"

"Why? You're not that amazing."

"Thanks a bunch," laughed Tammie.

Daniel backtracked hastily. "No, I mean you *are* amazing... " He stopped again, realising he'd dug himself into an even bigger hole. "What I mean is, people have been raised from the dead before. Mighty men of God from the past were able to do that kind of thing. Elijah."

"Yes, and Elisha."

"Exactly. And even Jesus himself had already done it, before you. There was a widow in one of the villages - John told me. Her only child. This young guy was in a coffin; they were actually carrying him on the way to his funeral - can you imagine?"

Tammie's eyes widened. She could just about imagine how extraordinary that must have been, and how they must have felt - especially the young man's mother. She was also quite glad she hadn't got as far as a coffin. Or a tomb. Eeugh.

"What *is* amazing is the forgiving of sins," Daniel went on. "No one's done that before."

"The Rabbis are saying only God can forgive sins," said Tammie.

"They've got a point, don't you think? You can forgive someone who does something bad to *you*. Like when Dibs set fire to a month's worth of my homework."

"Or when I pushed her and she crashed into you, and spoilt your Sabbath clothes."

"Was that you?" said Daniel, distracted for a moment. Ooops. He looked as if he might get annoyed, but then remembered he was trying to explain something really important. "Anyway - it's not easy, but you can choose to do it. But what right do you have to forgive things they did against someone else? You wouldn't even know about most of it. How can you forgive *everything* a person has done? Even their thoughts.

Because Jesus says that to think something is the same as to do it."

"Yikes," said Tammie - the thoughts of the last few hours and minutes and seconds starting to replay alarmingly in her head.

"Who has the power to do that?" continued Daniel. "Some people say Jesus is just nice and kind, but I don't buy it. Thinking he has the right to forgive sins? - that's not a 'good' person. Either he's a complete nutter, or he's the most insufferably arrogant person who ever lived, or... " Daniel trailed off in wonder. "Or he really can forgive sins, in which case he's different. Totally different. Greater than anyone we've ever had."

There was more and more about this Jesus to take in, thought Tammie. It gave her butterflies in her stomach. "I wonder what God might have sent him to do?" she said in awe.

"Jesus says he's come to fulfil the Law and the Prophets," said Daniel. "Not just obey them; not carry on from them. *Fulfil* them."

Tammie gasped, and a rush of goosebumps shivered across her. Daniel was right - no one had claimed this kind of thing before. She wasn't quite sure what it meant, but it sounded huge. Then she landed back down to earth, remembering what she'd just witnessed. She swung round to cross-examine Daniel.

"What's with the talking to trees?"

He smiled, slightly embarrassed.

"I've always kind of wanted to be a teacher, like your father. Telling people about God. But I'm supposed to be a fisherman; that's what my family's preparing me for. It's what we've always been. Now though, well - things are changing. Jesus is a carpenter. And his closest followers are all sorts. I've been practicing, just in case maybe one day I could be like them. I write down what Jesus says when he teaches the crowds - as much as I can, anyway - then I have a go."

"You've been writing down what Jesus says?" cried Tammie, desperate to hear. "Tell me!"

"OK, you sit here," said Daniel, quickly whipping out his scroll again. "This was from the other week, when we were up on a hillside. I'll start it again from the beginning."

He moved further up the grassy slope, then hesitated.

"Was it really you who ruined my Sabbath tunic?"

"Yes. Sorry. So what did Jesus say on the hillside?"

Daniel sighed, deciding to let all thoughts of mangled clothing go. It wouldn't help him preach a sermon about forgiveness if he wanted to clock Tammie. And given that they had so nearly lost her, a bit of fabric probably wasn't that important.

"You've got to imagine loads and loads of people," he explained. "Really mega. Too many to be able to see and hear Jesus properly. So he goes further up the hill, then everyone gets a chance to listen. Though some people near the back still misheard a bit - it was quite funny."

Daniel took a last glance at the scroll as a reminder, and Tammie clasped her knees in anticipation.

"Ready?" He sat down in the way Rabbis did, arms outstretched to invite the crowd's attention, and started speaking loudly and confidently:

"Blessed are the poor in spirit, for theirs is the Kingdom of God. Blessed are those who mourn, for they shall be comforted. Blessed are the meek and humble, for they shall inherit the earth. Blessed are those who hunger and thirst for righteousness, for they shall be filled. Blessed are the merciful, for they shall be shown mercy. Blessed are the pure in heart, for they shall see God. Blessed are the peacemakers, for they shall be called the children of God. Blessed are those who are persecuted because of righteousness, for theirs is the Kingdom of God.... "

Chapter Twelve

A BROTHER AT LAST

It wasn't too long before Tammie got her chance to be part of one of Jesus's massive teaching sessions for real. Massive in length, and in the sheer number of people who attended - some of them weren't even from Galilee or Judea. Was this what it was always like, being around Jesus? Crazy. There was Jesus himself, sitting in the main room of Simon's house (who Tammie kept having to remind herself to call Peter), with people crammed in all around him, and the doors and windows wide open and people packed all around them. Rebekah had long given up trying to be hospitable. It would have been hard for her even to reach most of the crowd, let alone offer them drinks and nibbles.

Tammie herself was outside, right on the edge, trying to hear through an open side door. Dibs quickly bored of it, skimming stones across the lake because they couldn't make out much of the conversation - but Tammie found it very interesting just to watch people's attitudes and responses reflected in their bodies.

Jesus was as relaxed as when he addressed the small gathering in Tammie's home. He spoke calmly, but there was great confidence under everything he did. Not a pushy, showy kind of authority that you see in some important people; just the quiet kind that comes when someone knows exactly what they're talking about, and doesn't feel scared of anyone.

Then there were the ordinary people: some hanging on his every word, like Simon Peter and John - some hanging back, like Thomas - but all rather confused. And then the scholars, the teachers like her father; not just ones she knew from the surrounding towns, but many more. Jairus listened steadily to Jesus, but others rippled with irritation. It was clear to Tammie that they didn't like having to stay still and listen to someone else. Why did they come, she wondered, if they didn't want to hear Jesus speak? It was as if some powerful fascination was both drawing them and trying to push them away.

Every now and then they broke out in annoyance, besides themselves and unable to contain it. On one occasion, Tammie caught something about the devil. What was all that about - had someone accused Jesus of working for him? Jesus's followers looked shocked, but Jesus answered evenly. He didn't seem to need time to gather his thoughts, he already knew his reply. Clearly he didn't try to tone it down, because the Rabbis erupted in fury. Tammie had often watched heated debate, where teachers wrangled over the details of God's law, but this was very different. There must have been a big shift while she was ill. And, somehow, it must all be to do with Jesus.

Still the crowd grew. Looking around, wondering where they would all go, Tammie spotted a middle-aged woman arrive with four younger men. They stood out to her because she had been guessing people's attitudes from their faces and bodies, and this group didn't belong together. The woman had a quiet assurance, calm and unhurried, and the men - her sons, presumably - were fidgety and cross. The woman caught Tammie's eye and smiled.

Tammie had been brought up to be polite to strangers, especially those who weren't in the first flush of youth, shall we say (although this lady was a bit hard to pin down in age; she had a timeless quality). They'd connected, if only by a glance, so Tammie reluctantly decided she'd better leave her spot near the side door and go and be useful, though she didn't quite know how. She could welcome them to Capernaum, at least.

She was just drawing breath to do so, when the oldest of the men snapped his fingers and shouted to her:

"You, girl!"

Well, that was rude. His mother frowned at him.

"Jamie."

Tammie found it hard to stifle a grin, seeing his reaction to being told off in public - and with a childhood version of his name, not the proper one. He mustered his dignity to ignore it, and carried on ordering Tammie about.

"We're here to see our brother. This is all getting out of hand; crowds of people - he can't even eat properly. We've come to take him home."

"*I* haven't," said his mother. Quietly. Firmly.

That's who she reminded Tammie of! Jesus. That calm authority, if not quite as strong as his. That ability to stay on track, when people around you are getting rattled and trying to knock you off course. So this was Jesus's family. Everyone has to have one, Tammie supposed - though they weren't quite what she expected. And what on earth was the small town of Nazareth doing for chairs and doors, with a whole family of carpenters off wandering the countryside?

"Tell him his mother and his brothers are here to see him," commanded the man Tammie would forever think of as Jamie.

Tammie nodded with as much courtesy as she could and turned to face the house. This was going to be a project. Getting in, for a start off; but then telling Jesus what to do. She'd seen enough of him to know he would act as he decided, regardless of other people's wishes. Oh, well; that wasn't her problem. She was just the messenger.

She started squeezing, wriggling and shimmying through any space she could - like some kind of weird dance - creatively weaving up and under and through; breathing in to slip into the smallest gap. She got to the main door and positively flattened herself to the dimensions of a slice of bread as she slid through, round the frame, and ended up pinned against the wall by the crush of people.

Tammie caught her breath, wondering how she would get Jesus's attention - but there was no need. He looked straight over and stood up so she could see him better, waiting. A new dilemma hit Tammie - speaking in front of all these people! No; she was just speaking to Jesus. That was all that mattered.

"Your mother and brothers are outside, wanting to see you," she said, watching for his reaction: an almost unnoticeable narrowing of the eyes. Tammie couldn't resist. "Jamie," she added. A tad more narrowing, with just a hint of a grin. Slightly reproving, perhaps? Slightly amused, definitely.

Jesus looked around. "Who are my mother and my brothers?" he asked.

What a strange question. Tammie wasn't the only one to think so, as people glanced at each other, wondering where he was going with this.

"Here they are," he said, gesturing to Peter, John and others seated on the ground around him; Caleb, leaning on his staff in a corner; Daniel and the other lads squashed up near the ceiling, perched on the rickety ladder leading to the roof. "Whoever does the will of my

Father in heaven is my brother. And my mother," he threw a look to Old Sarah and Rachel, peeking in from Sarah's room. Then he took in Salome... Rebekah... Naomi... Tammie. "And my sister."

Tammie gasped, unable to believe it. Seriously? After all these years of longing for a brother or sister - was he really saying that he was her big brother? The most wonderful person she'd ever met - someone she felt a little in awe of - someone who hardly even knew her, with all the others crowding in for his attention - and he wanted to be her brother?

Even though she now had an enviable position, right there in the room, Tammie barely heard much else as she tried to take it in. There was something from the Rabbis about wanting a sign to prove who he was, but Jesus said they would only be given one sign. Like Jonah was in the fish's belly for three days, so the Son of Man would be three days in the belly of the earth. No - that couldn't be right, could it? Tammie tried to stop thinking about the brother/sister thing and concentrate more on what Jesus was saying.

But soon everyone was moving, as Jesus suddenly went to the door. Surely he wasn't obeying his brother's demands?

Clearly not. He walked through the crowd to the water's edge, just exchanging a little look with his mother, and waded through the shallows to Peter's boat, clambering in. It seemed a bit random to Tammie, but the crowd appeared to know what was going on. This had obviously happened before. Peter also got into his boat and paddled out just a little way, while everyone else arranged themselves along the shoreline, on the roofs of the surrounding houses and even up palm trees.

Daniel, his brothers and other fishermen took some out in their boats on either side (Daniel trying frantically to jot down some of what he'd missed while clinging to the ladder). There was suddenly plenty of room for everyone to see and hear Jesus - although most of the Rabbis strode off, now they were no longer in a position of honour.

This was more like it. Tammie settled down at one side of the crowd, where she would be able to hear every word. She noticed that Jesus's mother had made herself comfortable nearby, sitting on an upturned boat, waiting with pleasure to hear her son - though his brothers could barely contain their frustration.

Tammie wasn't disappointed; it was enthralling. Even Dibs came over to listen properly. Jesus had a way of explaining things in stories, that made it more like a game to understand what he meant. Sometimes people would ask him questions, but most of the time they just listened. The stories were about their everyday lives - a funny one about lighting a lamp and then putting a bowl over it so no one could get any light from it. How pointless would that be? And one about how the tiniest speck of a mustard seed grew into a tall tree with branches that spread everywhere, and gave shelter to many. And one about a farmer sowing his grain and it landing all over the place, so that only some of it grew. He looked at Dibs's father Tobias as he told that one, and Tobias nodded. As a farmer he could understand that problem very well.

It went on for hours, but Tammie still wanted more when he finished. Simon Peter brought the boat back in, and lots of people paddled into the water before Jesus had even climbed out, stopping him getting back to the shore. He stood with them in the warm shallows, and Tammie realised they were bringing him people who were ill. She had been in no position to appreciate her own miracle, what with being dead at the time, so she watched with fascination as person after person went to him empty, weak and sad and left full and whole, overflowing with joy. It happened so many times it almost felt normal after a while.

Tammie noticed that Jesus's mother was also watching him closely. She seemed nice, so Tammie plucked up courage to speak.

"I love the way he tells stories," she said. "Stories are great. My dad is really good at telling them."

"I think Jesus gets it from his Dad too," said Jesus's mother. She smiled to herself, enjoying some private joke.

When everyone had been to him who wanted to, Jesus waded to land and headed over to his mother. He kissed her forehead, she picked a stray thread from his tunic, and they gazed into each other's eyes and talked as if no one else were near - while his brothers stood there in a huff, arms folded.

As Jesus hugged his mother goodbye, 'Jamie' drew breath to speak, doubtless about to command him to come home. But Jesus stepped in first, totally in control.

"I'm going across to the other side of the lake, now," he said, and his brothers somehow didn't dare argue. "Don't try to set off home until tomorrow. There's a storm coming."

"Rubbish," muttered one of the brothers, as they surveyed the sky in disbelief. Actually, he didn't say 'rubbish', but that's the politest way I can translate it.

Jesus indicated Tammie, to her surprise. "Tammie will help you find somewhere to stay."

Tammie stuttered some kind of agreement, thrilled that he had thought of her, and waved him off as he and his closest followers got into Peter's boat and struck out from shore.

The rules of hospitality in that part of the world meant that Tammie should invite them to stay at her house, but a far better plan popped into her mind. Who did she know with a huge house which had been empty and lonely for so long?

"Salome!" she shouted across the crowd. "You have a guest room, don't you?"

"Oh - yes!" came the response, as Salome rushed over to them and greeted Jesus's mother. "Yes, I have a lovely guest room. It's light, and very comfortable, and it's done out so prettily. Please, would you stay with me? I have other rooms, too. Plenty of space for your sons."

"My brothers and I do not require lodgings," said the eldest, a tad haughtily. "Thank you," he added as an afterthought.

"Whatever you wish," said Salome, leading them away, as the sun was nearly setting. "I also have a courtyard. We can't have you sleeping in the street!"

It was as Tammie got ready for bed that she remembered what Jesus had said about a storm on the way. She felt quite odd, and quickly snuggled up under her covers. Some time later she awoke to distant thunder, and then the full fury hit the small town. This happened sometimes - a sudden storm out of nowhere, sweeping across the lake. But this one was particularly violent.

Tammie didn't even feel smug that Jesus's brothers had been proved wrong and were caught in it. She was glad they would be able to hammer on the door and take refuge in Salome's house; no one should be outside in this. Had Jesus reached the other side of the lake yet? Tammie sincerely hoped so. But in a way, it didn't matter. Jesus had known the storm was coming; he could be trusted. He wouldn't have told his followers to sail to the deep water if he hadn't known that they would be safe.

It was frightening, even lying in her bed, as lightning smashed to earth with a mighty crack, and the wind ripped at the house. Tammie curled up tight, terrified, gripping her blankets, hardly daring to breathe.

"Please help!" she whispered, as another crash of thunder jolted her body. Who was she talking to? She didn't even know; it was automatic. But it worked.

The storm calmed immediately, and the sensation of peace that followed was more intense than anything Tammie had ever felt. She wanted to puzzle over what had just happened; she wanted to work out how it was possible, and who could have heard and answered her cry for help in the middle of such chaos. But such was the stillness and complete security inside her, all she actually did was drift off into the most wonderful sleep.

Chapter Thirteen

CALLED TO FOLLOW, BUT
CALLED TO STAY

As Tammie settled back into life at Capernaum, it was obvious things were never going to be quite the same. The arrival of Jesus had made such an impact that, whatever you felt about him, you could never ignore the change that had been made.

Sometimes Jesus and his closest followers were off on a journey, travelling round towns and villages. At those times Capernaum was missing many of the well-known faces everyone had taken for granted, and the town seemed quite empty and listless. Then word would come that Jesus had been sighted, and the huge crowds would pour back again from far and wide, bringing sick people for him to heal, and clamouring to hear him preach.

There was a change in people's attitudes too; the respect Jairus had enjoyed wasn't the same. Jesus's followers naturally looked to Jesus himself for leadership, and those who were against him were puzzled or even angry to think that their Rabbi approved of him. What upset Tammie most was when a group of people from the town, whom they had always been fond of, came to speak with her father.

"The man is a blasphemer, Rabbi; he's against God!" said Reuben, with great concern on his old face. "You said so yourself, to begin with. You've always been such a good servant of the Lord; it hurts us to see you being deceived."

"And to see a learned man like you, sitting being

taught by a common working man - it's not right," added Reuben's wife. "If he was from God, he wouldn't have ideas above himself. He'd be content to do the work his father does, and not bring shame on his poor mother."

"We have all been waiting for God to send us his Messiah, his Annointed One," said Jairus very gently. "That has been the hope of our people throughout the centuries, hasn't it? That God would send us a great King and Priest from the line of King David, who would win the victory for us and sit on David's throne forever. My whole life has been spent preparing the people in my care for that time, when God would fulfil his promise and send us his chosen one. If that time has now come, then my job is completed. My purpose has been served."

"How can you say such things, Rabbi?" asked Reuben, close to tears. "Are you really telling us to believe that this... this carpenter is the Holy One of Israel?"

"No," said Jairus. "That is something which every man, woman, girl and boy must decide for themselves. I would never ask you to believe in Jesus because I say so - it would mean nothing. You must each come to your own conclusion before God. I have come to mine."

And the honest, decent people went sadly away, bitterly regretting the change in their beloved Rabbi. They still attended the Synagogue and listened respectfully to Jairus as he taught, but you could tell that deep inside they had given up praying for him.

Although Tammie had loved the peaceful, cosy life she had before, she couldn't regret the changes. She had come to know Jesus, and that more than made up for the invasion of the masses, or the comments and stares from a few children who used to be her friends.

It was frustrating having to stay at home when Jesus was leaving town; she longed to be able to join those who went around with him, listening to his teaching and looking after him. Daniel felt the same way, if not more so, since his brothers were part of Jesus's closest team. Even Daniel's mother would sometimes travel around, when the group included Jesus's own mother and sisters, and some of the women Jesus had helped.

One day Salome stopped to talk hastily with Tammie as she rushed along the street, obviously in the middle of important preparations.

"Oh my dear," she gasped, "you'll never guess. I'm going with him! I've been talking with some of the other women, and it suddenly hit me that maybe I could join them!"

Tammie heard this with great pleasure, and Daniel came running over to listen too.

"You're going to travel with Jesus?" he asked eagerly, and then added as an excuse for his interest, "I'll tell my mother; she'll be pleased to have you along."

"Tell your parents for me too, Tammie dear," said Salome. "This is all so sudden, I won't have time to say my goodbyes."

"Oh, this is just perfect!" said Tammie hugging her. "This is just the right thing for you to do, I know it."

"Yes, I feel that too," said Salome. "I can't think why it never struck me before. I had nothing - nothing at all - and he gave me everything. All I want is to give him everything back. I've been to ask him, and he just smiled and said yes."

"No more skulking around in the crowd, afraid to talk to him?" laughed Tammie.

"No. No more skulking. Well, goodbye my dears. I must go and get ready, we'll be leaving soon."

She hurried off in excitement, and Tammie and Daniel watched her go with very mixed feelings. Her news was wonderful, but they wished they could go too. Daniel suddenly set off walking resolutely in the direction of the lake.

"Where are you going?" asked Tammie, running to keep up.

"To find Jesus," he said with great determination. "She said they were going soon. Come on."

They found Jesus near Simon Peter's boat on the shore, surrounded by people saying goodbye. He looked too busy to disturb, and Daniel hesitated a moment afraid that his brothers would shoo him off. Jesus turned and saw Tammie and Daniel, and gave them a wave. Soon he made his way over to them, and they walked a little aside from the crowds.

"Have you come to say goodbye?" he asked kindly after a pause, as Daniel was too tongue-tied to say what was on his mind.

"No," said Daniel. He gulped a few times, then blurted out "Please can I be one of your followers?"

"But you are already," said Jesus. "I've counted you as one of my truest followers since I first came here."

"Really?" said Daniel, going pink round the edges. "Well... can I come with you then, like my brothers? You said yes to Salome, will you say I can too?"

"No, Daniel. I need you to stay here."

Daniel hung his head and sighed. "I'm too young, I suppose. When will I be old enough?"

"It isn't anything to do with your age. I call different people to different jobs, and they're all just as important. And I always pay for what I take. Do you remember when I first came here? I used Simon and

91

Andrew's boat to preach from, and I called them and your brothers to follow me. But before we left there was an enormous catch of fish, so that your family and theirs had plenty to live on while the men were away."

"That's true, Rabbi," admitted Daniel. "We still have a little money left from that catch."

"And Simon Peter's wife, looking after her children all alone when I take her husband away? I gave her back her mother, so she's not alone. I'm giving you to your father in the same way. You will fill the place of your brothers, and your family will not lose as a result of helping me."

Daniel hadn't looked at it that way before. He saw himself as very grown-up and responsible all of a sudden, rather than a kid left at home because he would be of no use. He felt honoured, yet somehow not good enough at the same time.

"I'm not sure if I can fill the place of James and John," he said, a little worried. "There's two of them, and they're stronger than me."

"I'm not stupid," smiled Jesus. "I never call anyone to something without giving them the ability to do it. So do you feel happy now?"

"Yes. Yes, it's funny, but I do," said Daniel with a new look of certainty in his eyes.

"And what about my other disciple?" asked Jesus. "Do you want to run away with my trusty band?"

"No," said Tammie, "not now."

"Good," said Jesus. "I didn't give you back to your parents to snatch you away again so soon. And anyway, while we're away telling people the good news of the Kingdom of God, who will tell it to the people of this region, if you all come with me?"

"Yes, and who will keep an eye on Dibs to make

sure she behaves herself?" said Tammie. "That's a very responsible job. I'll need a great deal of ability for that."

"I'll give it my urgent attention," said Jesus.

Tammie and Daniel felt happier to wave the group off each time after that, knowing that they were being left rather like a garrison of soldiers in a fortress, keeping the work going, while the advance guard went ahead pioneering. But it still didn't help quite enough during those long, dreary days as the rainy season dragged on and on, and even Hezekiah the Toad looked as if he would welcome a dry spell. Jesus hadn't been back for ages, and Tammie began to wonder if perhaps he had decided to go and live somewhere less soggy, and not bother with his short and enthusiastic young helpers in an obscure fishing town, somewhere at the blunt end of the Mediterranean.

Chapter Fourteen

INTIN... ITRIN... ITE... WANDERING FOLLOWERS

It was on such a day as that, when Tammie got up and looked glumly out of her window, gazing at the sky and wondering whether this really *was* the end of the rainy season or the blue bits were just having her on, when Daniel and Joel came tearing into the courtyard. They were bringing news that Jesus had been seen again, running round and telling all his followers.

"We saw the boat," explained Daniel breathlessly, "and there's lots of people passing through the town. They're all following the boat round the shoreline, because no one knows where he's going."

"I expect he's trying to get away from the crowds," said Jairus. "There's been sad news. Do you remember his cousin John, the baptiser, who used to preach out in the desert?"

"The one Andrew used to follow, before Jesus came," said Daniel.

"Yeah, the one who lives on insects and never brushes his hair. My dad says he's a loon," added Joel, then remembered where he was.

"I think 'delusional' would be a nicer word," murmured Naomi, her face as pained as if she'd just eaten an insect herself.

"A lot of people thought that about him, however you want to put it," said Jairus. "Well, I'm afraid King Herod has had John killed. It's a great shock. Herod's such a coward, and he seemed to believe John was from God, even though he never took any notice of what he said. I did think John was safe, even in prison. It must have hit Jesus hard. I expect he's sailing across the lake hoping to lose the people and land somewhere quiet."

"Oh," said Daniel, his face falling. "We were going to go with the crowds and meet him where he landed. But I suppose if he wants to be by himself, we shouldn't go, should we?"

Jairus and Naomi looked at each other, and it was obvious that they wanted to go too.

"The crowds will be there *anyway*... " said Naomi.

"Yes," said Jairus. "And it might be a comfort to him to have real friends among them. So many just follow him around hoping to see a miracle."

"If Jesus is sad, I want to be with him," said Tammie, and everyone agreed.

The boys rushed off again, and Naomi hurriedly gathered some food, as none of the family had had breakfast yet.

"We'll eat as we go; we don't want to get left behind," she said. "Now Rachel, are you sure you don't mind? Do you think you can manage?"

"Off you go," said Rachel, herding them to the gate like chickens. "Goodness me, what a fuss."

People were already joining the crowds, all milling around, and a holiday mood was in the air. Tammie had to wait a little while Dibs got herself and Jake ready - she'd been having a lie-in, needless to say. As they ran along the shore they came across Daniel, who was at the door of his house, having some difficulty getting away from his mother.

"Now you wait your hurry," Susanna was saying as she packed a bag for him. "There's no need to go tearing off, then regretting it later when you've had nothing to eat. Good job I had a big bake. Who knows where you'll be going, and how long you'll be away?"

"Good morning," said Tammie as they came to the door.

"Good morning, girls," said Susanna. "There you are, Daniel, you aren't the last. Now maybe you won't be in such a fidget to be off. Go and get me a piece of soap, will you? We can wrap it in a cloth."

Daniel slunk back into the room to get what she wanted, and Susanna carried on in a leisurely manner.

"So you're all going, are you? Well I'm sure Jesus will be pleased to see you. Especially Daniel. He's very fond of my boys, is Jesus. James and John are particularly close to him, of all the twelve main disciples; I daresay you've noticed?"

"Er, yes," said Tammie politely. "He seems to like them very much."

"Oh, he does," said Susanna with satisfaction. "People often say to me that he's obviously training them to be the leaders of the group."

"Simon Peter seems to be the main one of the Twelve," said Daniel.

"Only because he's older," snapped Susanna. "Just you wait till your brothers grow up a bit more. 'Peter' indeed," she added to herself under her breath, as she stropped off to fetch more food.

"Jesus's nickname for James and John is 'Sons of Thunder,'" explained Daniel to the girls in a whisper. "She keeps worrying he means her!"

Tammie exploded with laughter, and managed to turn it into a cough. Susanna looked across at them suspiciously.

"Now don't just stand there, Daniel, get me the blankets from off your mat."

"I don't need blankets, Mother!" said Daniel, blushing. Tammie had noticed that he always went pink round the tips of his ears when he was embarrassed.

"You'll likely be gone at least till tomorrow; what will you do at night?"

"Roll myself up in my cloak, the same as everyone else. If I take blankets, I'll never keep up!"

"Have it your own way," said Susanna.

Daniel gave her a kiss and was about to leave, when she noticed a bit of dirt on his face and licked her handkerchief to rub it off.

"Mother, please... !" he protested, squirming, but she wasn't going to let him get away with dirt on his face. Tammie couldn't help smiling, but she pretended tactfully not to be looking. Dibs had no such inhibitions, and watched his discomfort with great glee. His ears were so purple now you could have toasted marshmallows at them.

At last they were off. Tammie took Daniel's bag so that he could carry Jake, and they raced away as fast as they could. It didn't take too long to catch up with the rest, and they settled down to enjoy the journey. The rains had cleared up for now, it was a beautiful March day (the month of Adar, in the Jewish calendar), and they were followers of Jesus who were travelling to be with him, just this once.

Tammie found her parents and munched at her breakfast as they walked. A lot of people who had joined at Capernaum seemed to be doing the same, they had decided to go on such a spur of the moment. The crowd walked on briskly and eagerly, and in time the boat seemed to be coming closer to the shore. The people pressed forward, and Jesus was surrounded soon after he landed.

He seemed tired, and though he smiled as kindly as ever, his eyes didn't smile. But in spite of his sorrow he spent time healing people, and talking to individuals in the crowd of thousands.

"It's because he loves people," thought Tammie as her eyes followed him around.

He came over to the group where Tammie was and embraced Jairus and Daniel warmly; Jakey wanted to be picked up to give him a kiss, and he didn't seem to mind at all. Tammie shyly put her hand in his free one and he gave it a squeeze.

"What would you like me to do for you?" he asked.

"Nothing, Rabbi," said Jairus. "We just wanted to be with you."

"We've come to help you, Jesus, instead of you always helping us," said Tammie. "We're very, very sorry about your cousin."

A stray tear dropped onto Jesus's beard.

"We make it all better," said Jake, gently wiping the tear away.

Then Jesus handed Jake back to Tobias, and went a little way up the hillside so that people could see him better, just like Daniel had shown Tammie. Everyone gathered round and sat on the grass, all lush after the months of rain.

He spoke to them for hours and hours, with more of his stories. He always seemed able to come up with new ideas. This time there was one about some bridesmaids running out of oil for their lamps, even though they knew the groom would probably be coming to collect them quite late. And there was one about a shepherd who cared about every single one of his sheep so much, he would notice if even one wandered off; he would look everywhere for it so he could carry it safely back - and then he would have a massive party to celebrate. And there was such a sad one about a man with a vineyard, whose own son was killed by the people who were supposed to be looking after it for him.

Tammie was so proud of Jesus as she listened, and saw all these adults lapping up his every word. Naomi and Jairus were just as keen to hear the stories as Tammie herself, and the time passed almost magically so that dusk was nearly on them before anyone realised, and everyone suddenly became aware that they were getting rather stiff - and *very* hungry.

Chapter Fifteen

SEVERAL THOUSAND INTO FIVE *WILL* GO

"Please may I have some more food?" whispered Tammie to her mother as Jesus finally stopped speaking.

"I'm sorry, darling," said Naomi, looking worried. "We left in such a hurry I only brought what I could lay hands on - and we've eaten it all for breakfast."

"I was going to slip off to a village to buy something, but it's all been so enthralling I simply forgot!" said Jairus. "I could go now, I suppose, but we're in a very remote place. Even if you come with me, it will be quite some time before we get anything."

"But we haven't eaten for hours!" said Tammie, beginning to feel rather alarmed.

All around, people seemed to be in the same position. Parents were looking concerned and little children were crying. Some people had been walking for days in the crowd, and had for a while been living only on what others could give them.

Jesus had been talking with his twelve closest followers, and some of them now came over.

"James,... " said Daniel.

"Not now please, Daniel. I'm busy," said James, bustling around being important.

"But I've got some food left, even though I shared lots."

"Of course!" laughed John. "We should have known Mother wouldn't let you leave the house without enough food for a fortnight!"

"Well done, Daniel," said Andrew. "But don't you want to keep it for yourself and your friends?"

Tobias was just opening his mouth to say that this was a very good idea, when Jake decided to use his nose as a handle to pull himself up on, so he was distracted for a moment.

"No, give it to Jesus. He'll know who needs it most," said Daniel, digging around in his bag. "There's not very much, I'm afraid. Just four little barley loaves, and a couple of fish. Oh, and another loaf."

Tobias watched with indignation as Andrew carried the food away, and Tammie herself couldn't help feeling disappointed, although she knew Daniel was right.

"Never mind," said Naomi to comfort her. "Other people might have some food left over too."

"Doesn't look like it," said Dibs, who had been standing up to watch the crowd. Everyone seemed glum, and the other disciples were going back empty-handed.

Then the instruction went out to get into groups of fifty or more, and sit together on the grass with a leader remaining standing.

"Now what?" muttered Tobias, as they all shuffled together. "This is no time for party games."

"I think Daniel should be our leader, don't you?" said Jairus. "As he's given up his food so generously."

So Daniel stood, with just the teeniest glow of pink about the ears, through pleasure not embarrassment this time.

Everyone was hushed with excitement, wondering what Jesus was going to do. It was very simple really - no flash of light, no voice from Heaven, nothing spectacular at all. He just held the food up and asked God to bless it, then started breaking it up and handing it to the Twelve, who in turn gave it out to the group leaders.

"Thank you," said Daniel, as James handed him some of his own food back. "What do I do when I've used this up?"

"Erm... just give this out, will you, then we'll see where we are," said James, who didn't seem to have an answer.

So Daniel began to give it out, very sparingly so that everyone would get a little - then round his group again, as there was still some left - and then again...

"I would leave the rest on your bag," said Jairus gently, as Daniel stood gazing in confusion at the food still in his hand. "We can help ourselves to seconds when we've finished this."

"Yes. Right," said Daniel, and he sat down and broke some off for himself, giving up trying to work it out.

Dibs wasn't going to admit defeat so easily; she watched the various group leaders like a hawk. A hawk with compulsive surveillance issues. But still she didn't manage to pin down exactly how it was being done - all she could really see was thousands of jolly people having a very large picnic together. Tammie just chomped away and grinned at Jesus. She didn't know how he had done it either, but understanding how it was done didn't seem at all necessary to enjoying the food.

"Has anyone got any water?" joked Jairus. "I could just do with a nice cup of wine to go with this."

"One miracle at a time; don't be greedy," smiled Naomi, and Tammie laughed. She'd caught up with all Jesus's earlier goings-on by now, so she knew about the wedding feast where they'd run out of wine. Nightmare. But then Jesus transformed gallons and gallons of water meant for cleaning into the best wine ever. Talk about abundance! Though she did wonder how they'd done the washing up.

Everyone ate as much as they wanted; there was no need to worry about being polite and leaving some for the others. They just carried on passing food to each other and helping themselves, until at last they all felt absolutely satisfied. Even Dibs.

"I expect what's happened is that people were hanging on to their food because they were afraid of going without," mused Tobias. "When Daniel was willing to share his, it kind of encouraged them, and they all started getting theirs out too. Yes, that'll be it, don't you reckon, Rabbi?"

"I'm a very simple man," said Jairus. "I can only come to conclusions on what I know. Among the sixty or so that we have here, I never saw anyone take food from anywhere other than what we were given. Did you?"

"Well, no," said Tobias, wondering why Jairus wasn't helping him out here. "I'm just saying, that's what must have happened."

Tammie couldn't resist.

"And do you think it's likely that everyone just happened to have left over exactly the type of bread and exactly the type of fish that Daniel had?" she asked innocently.

Naomi frowned at her so she didn't pursue the point, but hugged her knees and looked at Tobias to see how he would reply. He opened his mouth but couldn't think of anything in answer to that, so decided that as it was only a child who had said it, he was safe just ignoring it.

While everyone was getting up, stretching and brushing crumbs off themselves, Jesus handed a basket

103

each to the Twelve, who were looking around at the well fed people with considerable surprise.

"What's this, Rabbi?" asked Simon Peter.

"For the leftovers," said Jesus, pretending to be very serious. "We don't want to waste anything, do we?"

And he winked at Tammie, Daniel and Dibs as, in complete bewilderment, his men started collecting up the bits strewn all over the place. "What are we going to do with it all?" Tammie could hear them whispering to each other, as their baskets got fuller and fuller.

"Several thousand people," Thomas was saying to himself as he mulled it over. "At least four or five thousand men - call it five - and some with wives, plus all these kids - say fifteen thousand, and all in groups, which would make... Fifteen thousand, in groups, that's.... "

"Two hundred groups, at an average of seventy five per group," chipped in Matthew helpfully.

"Two hundred groups," said Thomas, lost in thought and completely unaware of Matthew. "So, two hundred group *leaders*, each being given a share of five loaves and two fish, which makes.... that makes.... "

"One fortieth of a loaf, and a hundredth of a fish," said Matthew promptly, to everyone's great amusement.

"....and a hundredth of a fish," continued Thomas, still under the impression he was working it out himself. "So..... "

"So each person getting one seven thousand and five hundredth of a fish, and one three thousandth of a loaf," concluded Matthew without batting an eyelid.

Thomas stood and shook his head while considered this.

"Hmmm," he pondered, blissfully ignorant of the audience he was attracting. He stooped again and carried on with the work. "Course, not all the men brought their wives, and kids don't eat much, so let's call it seven thousand. So. That's seven thousand people, all in groups.......... "

"Get back in the boat now, and head across the lake," Jesus said when they had finished clearing up. "I'm going to say goodbye to the people, and spend a little time by myself. I'll catch you up later."

So Simon Peter and Andrew got the boat ready, and the others started climbing in.

"Goodbye - though we'll probably be in Capernaum by the time you get home," said John, shaking hands with Jairus. "Oh, and Daniel... " Daniel turned to listen; "when you stop to sleep, be sure and ask someone to tuck you in safe and warm. Did Mother pack you a teddie?"

Daniel hurled himself at him. There was nothing he could do but cringe when his mother embarrassed him, but he wasn't going to let his brother get away with it. He and John rolled over and over, knocking Thomas's basket flying - which set him fussing and clucking like an over-zealous housewife. John won, but only just.

Then the boat set off, and Jesus went further up the mountainside alone. The tiredness and sadness were beginning to show again.

"I expect he wants to be by himself with God," whispered Tammie to her mother.

The weather was quite windy; it looked as if the rains might be continuing soon, so Tammie's group decided to walk through part of the night if they could. They were all feeling strong and full of energy after their good meal, and they had Andrew's basket of leftovers to pick at if they wanted. The track was on high ground around the side of the lake; Tammie could see Peter's boat striking out into the middle. It was being buffeted quite a bit by the winds, and the Twelve were having to row to make any headway.

Late in the night, when the boat had disappeared into the gloom, Dibs stopped to look at something. Whenever someone stares, it always tends to make a small crowd gather and stare in the same direction to see what they're missing, so within a moment all the people in that little group were looking too.

It didn't take long to spot what Dibs had seen; there was a small, pale blob moving slowly but steadily out into the lake. Dibs was gazing at it in a mixture of terror and disbelief, and other people rubbed their eyes. They were all trying to shake off the distinct impression of what the blob was. It was strange the way the moonlight played tricks with the eyes, but it looked exactly as if.... it really was just like.... in fact even if *you* had been there, you couldn't have helped wondering....

They looked at each other, and though they could tell they were all thinking the same thing, no one dared say it out loud.

It was Jake who spoke first. He had been dozing in Tobias's arms, and when he woke, he naturally looked to see what was fascinating everyone else. When he saw, he started chuckling and pointed to the blob.

"It's Jesus. Look Daddy, it's Jesus!" he said with huge enjoyment. "Silly Jesus, he forgot to take a boat!"

Tobias was intensely embarrassed that it should be *his* child who voiced such a preposterous thing, and tried to shut him up - but Jake was not having that. He started jigging up and down, waving and shouting "Jeeesus! Jeeesus!" at the top of his voice (and the top of Jakey's voice was pretty loud).

It was amazing, but once you had begun to imagine that this blob really did look very much like a person, it was remarkably easy to think that a head on top of the blob had turned, and an arm had come up from the blob - and waved back. They all looked at one another again with open mouths, and again no one dared speak.

After a few moments more of watching the blob making good progress, they turned and continued their way, shaking their heads as if to clear their brains. A few people tentatively commented on how tired they all were, and how odd moonlight could be, and others agreed.

Jairus and Naomi stayed watching the blob a little longer, their arms round each other. Tammie just caught her mother whisper, as they straggled after the rest:

"Well - he said he'd catch them up!"

Chapter Sixteen

SORTING OUT THE SQUID

No one dared ask Jesus how he had got there ahead of them when they arrived the next day, though he smiled very mischievously and asked if they'd had a nice walk. Quite a few people asked Simon Peter why his clothes were sopping wet from the chest down when they had landed, but he didn't seem at all inclined to go into explanations (and if you want to know what I think happened, you had better read chapter fourteen of Matthew's book in the Bible, because I'm not going to tell you).

Those who had been left behind listened with wonder and glee to the travellers' tales.

"We shall have to invite him next time we have a dinner party," was Rachel's only comment, but you could see from the twinkle in her eye that she was as pleased with Jesus's exploits as anyone.

They all went to the Synagogue and Jesus carried on teaching them with more stories. Tammie loved to puzzle over them and try to work out what he meant. Nearly all the stories were about what 'the Kingdom of God' is like, and sometimes it was easy to understand, but sometimes it wasn't. Dibs was particularly confused when Jesus said that the Kingdom of God is like a fishing net.

"Smelly, and with lots of holes?" she whispered.

"No, no," said Tammie, who was beginning to get the hang of these parable things. "He means there are lots of different types of people - for God and against him - and they'll have to be sorted, like the fish in a net."

"Oh," said Dibs. "I hope I'm a squid."

One of his twelve closest followers asked Jesus who would be the greatest in the Kingdom of Heaven. A long time afterwards, Tammie realised that no one could remember who had actually said it. Naomi thought it had been Simon Peter; Dibs said it was John - but Tammie wouldn't have that. Rachel was convinced it was Judas, but she never had liked him. When Tammie asked Peter if he could remember, he just smiled and said "It doesn't matter; we had all thought it." Certainly the Twelve all looked pretty shamefaced as Jesus turned his steady gaze on them. Everyone froze, wondering what he was going to say.

He faced the gathering and held out his hand.

"Come here, Jakey," he said.

People stirred in surprise, but little Jake pattered up to the front taking everything in his stride. Jesus set him right in the middle of the Twelve, in one of the places of honour of the Synagogue.

"I hope his feet are clean," murmured Dibs's mother anxiously, as he stepped onto the expensive carpet at the front.

"Never mind that," said the down-to-earth Rachel. "Let's hope he's been to the toilet recently."

Dibs's mother buried her face in her hands at the very thought, while all the girls and women within earshot got a fit of giggles. The men, who sat on the other side, looked across to see what the hilarity from their wives and daughters was about, and the wives and daughters managed to straighten their faces and be very solemn.

Jesus waited till everyone was settled, then said, "Unless you change and become like a little child, you won't even get into the Kingdom of Heaven."

There was quite a flurry at this, and a few people seemed offended. Jesus didn't seem either upset or pleased by the reaction, he just carried on with what he was saying.

"So whoever makes himself humble, like this child, is the greatest in the Kingdom of Heaven."

Jake looked up unblinking into Jesus's eyes; he didn't seem to understand what wonderful things were being said about him. His mother sat with her mouth open; Dibs looked doubtful, as if she wasn't sure she wanted to go to Heaven if it was going to be full of people like her baby brother.

"If you welcome a little child like this," continued Jesus, "it's as if you are welcoming me. But anyone who hurts one of these little ones who believe in me - well, they'd be better off being thrown into the sea with a huge stone round their neck."

Tobias shifted angrily in his seat. He thought Jesus had said quite enough, and was telling him how to run his family. But Jesus carried on, as if he hadn't noticed. He knelt down and took Jake in his arms.

"You know," he said, "you shouldn't look down on these little ones. They have their own special angels in Heaven, who are constantly in the presence of my Father. He isn't willing that a single one of them should be lost."

He took Jake's hand and led him back to his seat, where Jake told everyone he'd got his own special angel.

Jesus was about to go on with the stories, when a group of people came bursting in. Tammie knew them from the day before; she had heard some of the ringleaders saying they were going to make Jesus King of Israel, and throw out the Romans.

They entered the meeting rowdily, pushing their

way to the front and making a great fuss of him. He just looked at them, in the way Tammie had seen him look a few times. The way she hoped he would never look at her.

"You're only following me because I gave you the food," he said. "You shouldn't care for that sort of food, but for the everlasting food I can give you."

"Well, do a miracle so we can believe you!" they said, all hyped up, expecting something amazing that they could tell their friends.

"How many miracles do you want?" Dibs began to say very loudly, before several hands were clapped over her mouth.

Jesus didn't get angry like Tammie or Dibs (or quite a few of the adults), he replied calmly. He told them that *he* was the eternal food he was talking about, and that his body was living bread which he would give to feed the whole world, so that people could live forever. Everyone in the Synagogue went quiet as they heard this; then people started muttering, wondering whether he wanted them to become cannibals. Gradually a lot wandered out, saying he was mad. Weird. Dangerous.

"That's sorted out the men from the boys," commented Rachel with satisfaction.

"They don't understand," said Jairus sadly. "We've been waiting for our Saviour for so long, and we've always expected him to be a great soldier who would set us free from our *earthly* slave-drivers. They can't see that there are much more important things at stake here."

Jesus put his hand on Jairus's shoulder.

"A man like this," he said to those who were left; "he has long been instructed in the truths of the Holy Writings, but he also takes hold of the fresh things I am teaching you now. He's like a householder who can bring from his storeroom both new treasures and old ones to give to you."

"Is he saying your dad's a good teacher?" whispered Dibs.

"Yes," said Tammie.

"Thought so," said Dibs, with the air of one who knew all about parables now.

Many of the people who used to follow Jesus turned away from that day, and there were arguments all over the town, - even between members of the same family, like Thomas and Tobias. Things were more difficult than they had been, and Rabbis and Priests would regularly come up from Jerusalem to question Jesus.

Tammie could tell that they were trying to trap him into saying something that would make the Romans angry, but she wasn't afraid because she knew he was much too clever for them. She wished they wouldn't stay at her house when they came, but they ignored her most of the time so it wasn't too bad. One or two of them weren't really against Jesus anyway, she suspected. Jesus had followers everywhere, even on the big Council in Jerusalem.

One night she heard her father talking with his friends from the Council, Joseph and Nicodemus. They spoke in hushed voices for fear of the other Rabbis, but as Tammie was bringing them a jug of wine she caught their conversation before they noticed her.

"...there is talk of a reward being offered for his life," Joseph was saying. "There is no doubt in Jerusalem that they want him dead. If they get a chance to take him when the crowds are not near, they will most certainly seize it."

Jairus put up his hand to silence him as he saw Tammie, and all three men turned to look at her. Joseph seemed afraid, as if she might be a spy.

"It's all right, Joseph," said Nicodemus. "This is the daughter of our host. Good evening, Tamar."

"Good evening, sir," said Tammie, trying to be polite as she put the jug on the low table in front of them. She managed a smile, but at the same time a tear escaped onto her cheek, which they must have seen even in the dimness of the single rush light. She couldn't help thinking of what Joseph had said. She knew without question that he had been speaking of Jesus. She turned to go, but her father, who always knew what she was feeling, stopped her.

"Tammie." She turned back and looked at him. He hesitated a moment to find the right words. "Jesus... is a very wise man. He understands the dangers better than any of us. He will always do what he knows to be right. You don't need to be afraid for him."

Tammie thought for a moment. "But you are afraid for him, aren't you?" she said.

The men exchanged glances.

"And for ourselves," said Nicodemus quietly. "It's a grave situation. The men who oppose Jesus are powerful, but he is wiser, and he controls the situation."

"I don't know what will happen," said Jairus looking earnestly at her, "but I promise you they will never be able to take him unawares." He smiled to reassure her. "So go to bed now, and don't worry!"

Tammie thought about that conversation a lot as the time went by, but everything seemed to be fine. Jesus avoided going to Jerusalem when he knew it was dangerous, or went very quietly so that no one realised he was there. He answered all their trick questions

113

cleverly, and Tammie was fairly convinced that he was safe - even if the uneasiness did creep back from time to time.

And so life continued, with Jesus at the centre of their thoughts whether he was around or not. Tammie heard him teach many more mind-blowing things - and saw lots more, too - but I can't tell you about them *all* here. John said, many many years later, that if you wrote down all the amazing things that Jesus did, the whole world would not have room for the books!

And John should know.

Chapter Seventeen

THE MOST SPECIAL MIRACLE

It was coming round to Passover again - the most important time of the year. Tammie was getting excited, though being very grown-up now (fourteen last birthday! Whoop-di-diddly-dooya) she pretended to be cool about it all. Everyone who saw her these days said how ladylike she was looking, though it was a constant source of annoyance that she seemed to have stopped growing - and Dibs, who was shooting up, was about to overtake her. The way Dibs behaved nobody would ever mistake *her* for a lady, so that was some consolation.

Only that morning, Naomi had been having a little word with Tammie (you know the way mothers do sometimes). It will probably surprise you, but Tammie was round about the right sort of age to get engaged. Different places and cultures have their own way of doing these things, and this is how it was in Galilee at that time. Because the boy and girl were so young, it was usual for the parents to help them choose - and this was why Naomi had brought the subject up in her tactful way.

Tammie concentrated very hard on the eggs she was counting, because of course it is important not to lose count - and if her face went the colour of a spray-tanned beetroot it must have been because counting eggs is such a strenuous business.

"He would have to be very nice," Naomi said. "Someone we know well. Near your own age. And he would have to be someone who loves God, like you do. One of Jesus's followers, too; that's important. Let's see. Do we know anyone like that?"

115

She looked at Tammie with that kind but knowing smile she had (another speciality of mothers). And Tammie looked steadfastly at the eggs which she had long lost count of, and thought of a boy who was really a young man, and whose ears went pink when he got embarrassed.

Naomi changed the subject and Tammie's face had a chance to get back to its normal temperature, - but you can imagine how she felt when, not long after, Daniel came bursting into their kitchen. Even Naomi gave a guilty jump, though she turned to greet Daniel. Tammie busied herself about, looking unconcerned, putting the broom in the oven and the dinner in the slop bucket. It was a good job Rachel wasn't there as she'd have guessed immediately, but Daniel didn't seem to notice. Maybe he was too busy hiding feelings of his own.

"Is the Rabbi here?" he asked. "I hope I'm not too late. Father says I can go to Jerusalem for the Passover. He feels too old for the journey, and as Mother and James and John are already there with Jesus, I was going to stay with him - but he says he'll be all right."

"That's the point of us staying behind," said Naomi, "to look after anyone on their own. He can celebrate the feast with us."

"That would be good; I'll tell him," said Daniel. "But has the Rabbi set off yet? Father says I must go in his party."

"Don't worry," laughed Naomi, "they're leaving tomorrow. You've time to go home and pack up some things. What would your mother say if we let you go all that way without your warm cloak?"

"You are lucky," sighed Tammie the next day, as she stood in the courtyard waiting to wave them off.

"I know," said Daniel. "Jerusalem at Pesach, with all the thousands of people gathered there. It's very special."

"There's something to make it even more special," said Tammie. "You know why I really think you're so lucky."

Daniel nodded. "Jesus is there," he said, beaming. "To be there with him, at the most holy time of the year. He'll be keeping a low profile, but hopefully we'll see him a few times. You never know - we may even hear him teach, right there in the city of King David! Oh Tammie, it's going to be wonderful."

"You must remember everything, and tell me about it when you get back," said Tammie. "Promise?"

"Of course I will," Daniel was saying, when they were interrupted by a loud and very pointed cough.

"Excuse me," said Jairus. "I hate to break things up, but we're about to leave."

Daniel hurried off to join the group that had formed, and Tammie gave her father a big hug.

"Have an amazing time, and a very safe journey," she said. "I'll climb up onto the roof and wave you into the distance."

"Oh, it's *me* you're here to see off, is it?" he asked mock innocently, and roared with laughter as she tried to shut him up, anxiously looking around to see if Daniel had heard. These parents could be quite a liability; she just hoped he wasn't tempted to drop hints on the journey.

The little group soon faded from sight, and Tammie gave up waving and sat in her corner on the roof, in the shade of the trees. Pesach in Jerusalem. Everyone always hoped to go there at this time of the year for the feast. The city and nearby villages would be packed with people, not just from Judea and Galilee, but also Greece, Rome, Asia Minor, Syria, Babylon, Egypt, Africa. Wherever Jews had scattered, you could be sure some of them would make it to Jerusalem for the festival. Tammie remembered the heat, the crowds, the growing excitement and the happy celebrations. Most sacred of all was the Passover meal itself, which God had given them as a reminder throughout the years of the way he had rescued them from slavery long ago, when they had been held prisoner in Egypt. It was the most special miracle he had ever done for his people, and that was why remembering it meant so much to them.

Tammie stopped her daydreaming and slipped back down to the courtyard. There was lots to be done in the few remaining days if they were to be able to take the week's holiday after the feast, which God had set out. Great activity was already underway, and Tammie joined Caleb in tending the animals and cleaning out their stalls. Benjamin had gone with Jairus to Jerusalem, but Caleb was feeling too old these days for jaunting and gallayvanting, as he called it.

All too soon it was the fourteenth day of Nisan, Preparation Day itself, and the bustle reached fever pitch. From dusk it would be the fifteenth, the first day of the Passover, and that is when the meal would be eaten. There was a frenzy of cleaning and scrubbing and planning and cooking. All over the country women would be burning any bread or dough with yeast in to get rid of it, and making the 'unleavened' bread, without yeast, used in this celebration. Men would be checking the lamb to be used tonight - it had to be perfect, without any blemishes. Those who'd gone to Jerusalem would be asking around for a guest room, as it was the custom for the people of Jerusalem to allow travellers to use any spare rooms they had. There would be a huge queue at the Temple; Jairus would probably be there now, thought Tammie, as she changed into her blue dress and clasped the precious belt on carefully. The men would be taking the lambs to be killed at the altar as a sacrifice to pay for their sins.

The sun got lower and lower in the sky, and everywhere people gathered together - in the villages, in the farm settlements, in the cities; in the homes of neighbours, in the homes of strangers; in tents on the hills around Jerusalem, in isolated groups on foreign soil. There was a hushed excitement over all God's people. The sun set. It was Pesach, the Passover, once again.

In the half-light of the oil lamps Tammie looked around at the small group gathered in her house. Everyone was wearing their sandals, and Caleb and Daniel's father, Zebedee, carried a staff each and wore their cloaks, with the ends gathered up and tucked into their belts. This was to remember the way the first Passover was eaten hurriedly, with the people all ready to flee the country before the night was over.

Caleb was representing Jairus as the host of the meal, so he said the opening prayer and blessed the first cup of wine, which was passed around everyone. Then they each took a sprig of herbs, dipped it in salt water and ate it; that stood for the tears which the people of Israel shed during their four hundred years of slavery in Egypt. Then Caleb broke the first of the little loaves of unleavened bread which would be eaten during the evening, and they passed it round. It was unleavened to remind them that when their ancestors left Egypt they had no time to wait for the dough to rise, so God told them to use no yeast.

Tammie swallowed slightly to clear her throat and then stood. Everyone turned to look at her, and she felt as she did every year what an honour it was to have a part to play in such a celebration. As the youngest person present it was now her job to ask the host about the feast. All over the land young people and even tiny children would be doing the same. Little Jakey would be standing and carefully remembering the words his mother had taught him; somewhere in or near Jerusalem, Daniel would be asking Tammie's father; and if Jesus was with his closest followers, then John would probably be asking the question and Jesus himself would be giving the reply.

"What does this ceremony mean?" asked Tammie.

Caleb answered "It is the Passover sacrifice to the Lord, who passed over the houses of the Israelites in Egypt and spared our homes when he struck down the Egyptians. We keep this vigil to honour the Lord because the Lord kept vigil that night to bring us out of Egypt with a mighty hand."

And he told the story of what had happened nearly one and a half thousand years before: how the Egyptian Pharaoh had ignored all God's messages to let the people of Israel go, in spite of all the plagues God had sent. How Pharaoh even made their hardship worse, driving them almost to death. How God had warned of one final terrible plague, to kill all the oldest sons - and the firstborn of all the animals too, but still Pharaoh wouldn't change his mind.

Then God had told his people to kill a lamb for each family that night, and to eat the meal just as everyone was now eating it. But first of all they were to sprinkle some of the lamb's blood around the door frame as a sign; when the angel of death saw that, he would miss that house and not let the plague fall on it. It was as if the blood of the lamb was spilled instead of the blood of the eldest son, who would otherwise have died. The people stayed safely huddled inside their houses until it was all over, and then they heard the heartbreaking grief of the Egyptian families.

At last Pharaoh allowed them to go free from the cruel slavery they had been under for so long, and God led them - and any Egyptians who wanted to belong to him - out of the country. But even then it was not over, because Pharaoh changed his mind and came racing after them with his chariots and soldiers.

The people of Israel were trapped between the army and the Sea of Reeds, and it was then that God did what no one could possibly have expected - he actually divided the sea into two piled up masses, with dry land in between for the people to walk across! You would have thought Pharaoh would have got the message by then, but still he wouldn't turn back. He tried to chase after them... just as all the waters came crashing back into place. The people of Israel were free at last.

The story was very familiar, but as they listened to Caleb tell it - with the dark night outside and the eerie, flickering twilight of the oil lamps - it was easy to imagine that God was moving across the land even now to save them.

They sang some psalms and drank from the second cup of wine, then it was time for the meal. Everyone was given a big portion of roast lamb, because none could be left till morning, and a sauce of bitter herbs was served with it to remind them of the bitterness of their slavery. Then there was more bread and wine, and more singing of psalms, and when Tammie finally went to bed late into the night, it was with the words of the 'Hallel' ringing in her heart:-

"For you, O Lord, have delivered
my soul from death,
    My eyes from tears,
    My feet from stumbling,
    That I may walk before the Lord
in the land of the living."

Chapter Eighteen

A SKY AS HARD AS STEEL

Tammie had a long, drowsy lie-in the next day. It was a holiday from all their hard work, and they were positively not allowed to do anything. Tammie intended to make the most of it. She got up in time for the special meeting at the Synagogue to praise God and thank him for the Passover. That was always the best meeting of the whole year. When it was over they all sauntered back to their homes, and Tammie lolled about in the courtyard feeling lazy.

She had been snoozing for a while when she suddenly woke feeling cold and uncomfortable. As she sat up, rubbing her arm to get rid of the cramp, she realised why she had become so cold. What had been a warm, bright courtyard with the sun at its height in the soft blue sky only half an hour ago was now desolate, frightening... and dark.

For a moment she just sat there feeling afraid, looking at the sky. It was as if she were unable to move. Finally she stood but was unsure what to do, where to go. She climbed the steps to the roof very cautiously and looked around. She had seen the landscape look bleak before - during a storm, or at dusk in winter - but this was very different. There were no birds, no people - no animals even, except a couple of goats tethered outside Dibs's house, who cowered together in fear. The sky was a dark, dark grey, yet she could see no clouds, and she couldn't even tell where the sun was meant to be. The lake mirrored the gloom above it, and the slight movement of the water seemed threatening and sullen.

She gulped and hugged herself in fear as she took it all in, then noticed a figure at a slight distance, looking up at the sky. It was Caleb. Tammie climbed slowly down the stairs again, and walked towards him up the road that led from Capernaum. Her legs felt heavy and wouldn't stop shaking; her teeth were chattering and her hands were icy cold.

As she drew near she struck off the road and made her way across the scrub land to where he was standing. He didn't look at her, he just kept staring at that dark sky, as hard as steel.

"What is it?" whispered Tammie, after they had stood like that for what seemed ages.

He shook his head. "I don't know," he said very simply. "I just feel as if all joy has gone out of the world."

They said nothing more. Eventually Caleb broke the silence.

"Better go home," he said. "You don't want to catch cold."

Tammie nodded and turned back, though she knew it was more than just cold that was making her shiver.

She crept in at the gate. Rachel had woken from her nap and was gazing from her window, and Tammie sat huddled near her. Soon Naomi came to join them, and throughout the afternoon a number of Jesus's friends gathered there, drifting in by ones and twos. They felt disturbed by the strange darkness and somehow wanted to be together, although barely anyone spoke.

Finally there was a slight yet strange rumbling – so quiet and distant Tammie thought it was more like a shudder deep inside her than a noise. The blue sky returned, and people in Capernaum began to enjoy the holiday again; but that group gathered in Tammie's house couldn't get rid of the unreal feeling the darkness had caused. Throughout the Sabbath that followed they stayed together, very quiet; each one thinking and wondering, each one hoping the foreboding of that darkened sun would leave them.

Tammie couldn't shake off the fear which had been there since she first woke to see the ugly grey sky. That secret conversation between her father and his friends kept coming back, - and every time she thought about Jesus she got a sick, uneasy feeling. The night after the Sabbath she lay staring at the ceiling, thinking that this was unbearable. She had disturbed Dibs more often than she could count by rolling over, sitting up or pacing up and down - Dibs, the invincible sleeper, made strangely sensitive by that ironclad sky.

It was no good. Tammie was obviously never going to sleep tonight, and it was now within an hour of the dawn: the first day of the week. She went listlessly to the window and opened the shutter to look out at the world, all drab and colourless, neither night nor day. She gazed up at the sky and wondered if God knew how she was feeling. He must do, but it didn't seem as if he did. She felt so alone.

As she stared unlooking at the sky above her, she suddenly noticed a pinprick of light. It was the morning star, twinkling down at her. She smiled up at it and felt comforted a little. All the other stars had gone, but this one was hanging on bravely. She stood like that, watching it and feeling hope return - however feebly - until at last the life and colour seeped back into the world, like the delicate tint of watercolours spilled across a grey map.

It was morning. The sun had risen.

The following days passed quietly, with the same mood of waiting and wondering hanging over them, but Tammie no longer felt so desperately afraid. They were all still together even after the festival week had finished, and although they prayed or sang a quiet hymn from time to time, people generally preferred to be alone. Even Dibs sat scrunched up in a corner by herself, frowning at the wall, and Jake was curled up on his mother's lap, uninterested in the toys Tammie had found for him. Rebekah's children were the same. It was as if they were all waiting and listening for something.

That was why, when they heard the distant footsteps running towards Capernaum one evening, they seemed so much louder than usual and they all looked up. The banging on the gate, when it came, was as loud as a rifle shot.

Tammie bit her lip so hard that the blood ran as she watched Caleb lift the bar. Her stomach turned with suspense as he heaved the gate stiffly open; then Daniel and Benjamin fell through and collapsed onto the floor.

Everyone stared at them silently, their worst fears leaping and dancing through their heads. The young men were covered in mud and sweat; their clothes were ripped. Benjamin had fallen to his knees and they could see that his face was bloated with weeping, and running, and lack of sleep. Daniel was face down, gasping; he didn't look as if he cared if he ever got up again.

Caleb was the first to move. He closed the gate once more then fetched a pitcher of water, gently washing the dirt from Benjamin's face and offering him a drink. Benjamin shook his head weakly, but Caleb ignored him and carefully raised the cool liquid to his lips. Zebedee came forward and laid his hand on Daniel's shoulder, trying to comfort him. He stroked his hair, but Daniel seemed to know nothing of his father's touch. The old man sat down beside him and rolled him over so that he was cradled in his arms like a child. Daniel clung to him, and his sobs rent the courtyard, which was otherwise deathly quiet.

Tammie felt as if her heart and her head and her lungs would burst; as if she were being crushed. Everyone was standing around just staring. Nobody dared say anything. They didn't want to know the answer, so it was best not to ask. Jakey was the bravest. He stood up, looking straight at Benjamin, and asked the question that was filling everyone's mind.

"Where's my Jesus?"

Daniel cried out as if Jake had stabbed him with a knife, and gripped his father still tighter; Benjamin curled over in a ball and clasped his arms around his head.

Deep inside, every one of them knew that Jesus was dead, and each one felt that they had never known sadness till now. That question and its response released something, and one by one they broke down. All the pain and horror of it came flooding out of Tammie in noiseless sobs that shook her body savagely as if it would tear her apart. Naomi had half collapsed onto the floor, and Dibs seemed to be retching as if she would be sick, but Tammie couldn't even see anyone else. After a while the weeping subsided to a quiet murmur, then finally there was silence once more.

There was no hurry to get the details - what difference did it make? They sat or stood stony-faced, waiting for the two to be able to speak. It was like some kind of dream, something that wasn't real. It was as if life had stopped.

Nothing mattered. Jesus was everything; without him.... Tammie closed her eyes and leaned back against the wall. She wanted to faint. Why couldn't she faint? This pain was unbearable; she wanted everything to be blotted out. But no, she couldn't faint. She had to stay.

Chapter Nineteen

ALL OF US, IN SOME WAY

The young men recovered enough to tell what had happened, and bit by bit the whole story came out.

"It was Judas," said Daniel.

Benjamin shook his head. "It was the chief priests, too - and the Romans, and the people. It was all of us, in some way."

"But the people loved him," faltered Naomi.

"You'd think, wouldn't you?" said Benjamin. "At the start of the week they were hailing him as Messiah, then within days they were howling for his death." He closed his eyes as he remembered. "I've never seen a mob so full of hate. Terrifying."

"Tell us what happened, lads," said Caleb. "Try to remember."

"There was a plot," said Daniel, trying to take deep breaths. "Judas... "

"The Judas in his twelve closest followers?" asked Rachel.

"Yes. Judas sold him to the chief priests. They paid him to say when it would be easy to catch him, and to point him out to the guards. After the Passover meal they'd gone to one of the hills near Jerusalem; Jesus wanted to pray. I mean, he was *praying*.... "

He broke down again, and Benjamin took over.

"We didn't know anything about it at the time, but while Jesus was there with the Twelve - well, the Eleven I should say... anyway, while he was there praying, they sent this big group of Temple guards with Judas - all armed and everything, they were."

"Were none of our boys armed?" asked Zebedee.

"One or two were."

"Peter was," sniffed Daniel.

"Yes, Simon Peter was," continued Benjamin. "He attacked one of the guards. Sliced his ear off, but Jesus put it back and told his men not to fight. You know how he is. I mean.... " He couldn't bear to change it to 'was', so he trailed off lamely.

"So they arrested him," prompted Caleb, who seemed determined they should hear the whole story. Tammie's mind was swimming and she couldn't take it all in. Why hadn't Jesus seen the danger? Why hadn't he avoided it and stayed safe in Galilee? It would have been so easy.

"Yes," said Benjamin, pulling himself together. "They arrested him and put him on trial straightaway."

"In the middle of the night?" chipped in several people.

"That's against our laws," said Zebedee.

"Oh yes, the whole trial was a sham," said Daniel. "They had witnesses who made up stories, and none of the stories agreed... It was a complete mess."

Tammie gulped. "Did they try him at..... "

"It was the Council who tried him. The Sanhedrin," said Benjamin, knowing what she couldn't ask.

Tammie closed her eyes. Her father was a member of that Council. Naomi steeled herself to ask about Jairus, but no words came.

Benjamin and Daniel looked at each other.

"Well?" said Zebedee. "Did the Rabbi speak up for him at the Council? Did Jairus and his friends try to save him?"

"No," said Benjamin. "Nobody said a word for him, not one of us. Jairus went into hiding as soon as he got the summons to the Council meeting. It was the first we knew about the arrest - we were scared for our own lives. Later on, the next morning, the Roman Governor gave the crowd the choice between Jesus and some murderer; he said he'd let one of them go free. And none of us had the guts to ask for Jesus."

He hung his head in shame, and those who hadn't been there thought what it must have been like. They all knew they would have done the same.

"Even Peter let him down," said Daniel, glancing apologetically at Rebekah.

"Shush," interrupted Benjamin, "there's no need to tell that."

"Tell it all," said Caleb.

"While the trial was on, some girl recognised Simon Peter as one of Jesus's followers," said Daniel. "Peter swore blind again and again he didn't even know him. Said he'd never seen him before in his life." Rebekah was staring straight ahead, glazy-eyed. Daniel turned to her. "You must try to understand. Please don't blame him."

She nodded and gave a watery smile. "I don't," she said.

"But imagine how he must blame himself," murmured Old Sarah.

"You mentioned the Governor, Pontius Pilate," said a voice with a slight accent. It was the Roman centurion, Marcellus, who had become a follower of Jesus years before, when Jesus had healed his servant of the fever.

"Yes, Pilate put him on trial too," said Benjamin. "And King Herod. They were passing him between them for hours."

"If they wish to kill him, they would have to take him to the Governor," explained Marcellus. "Rome allows the provinces to keep many rules and customs -

but death, no. If the Council pass sentence of death it must go to the Governor, and he will try the case again."

It all went quiet. Nobody wanted to hear what happened next. But once more Caleb pushed relentlessly on.

"So Pilate passed the sentence?"

"Eventually, yes," said Benjamin. "He tried to get out of it. He even... he had him flogged. Whipped with those scourges the Romans have." Marcellus covered his face; he knew what that was like. "I think he was hoping the Council would agree to let him go after that. But they wouldn't; nor the people. So he passed the sentence, even though he said Jesus had broke no laws. You should have seen the mob. There would have been a riot if he hadn't."

"What was the charge he used?" asked Marcellus. "He would have to put down some charge in the records."

"Treason, I think," said Daniel. "Treason against the Roman Emperor, because some of the people had said he was their King."

Marcellus went white. "Treason! But that would mean... The punishment for treason is crucifixion."

Benjamin nodded. "Yeah," was all he said.

A wave of horror went round, as real as if it had hit them in the face. They had all heard of crucifixion; trust the Romans to come up with a way of death like that, to terrify their slaves and keep their subject nations under.

"Dear God!" murmured Marcellus, and Dibs snuggled up to her mother, crying like a little child.

Caleb could hardly bear to continue, but he forced himself to ask one last question.

"Did you... did you see him die?"

"No," said Daniel. "I wanted to stay. I hadn't spoken out for him, I was too afraid - but I did want to be with him till the end. But James wouldn't let me. We thought they would be coming for us next, his followers. James and John were staying, and Mother wouldn't leave, but they said I must come home."

"He would have stayed," said Benjamin. "He was refusing to budge, so they ordered me to take him home; I had to fight him and drag him through the streets to make him go."

"It was getting on for nine in the morning when we were leaving," said Daniel. "The crowds were huge because of the Passover, and of course lots of people were gathering to see Jesus pass by, on his way to the execution. At one point it was solid, and we couldn't get any further. And then they came by - the soldiers, and two other prisoners.... and Jesus."

Tears rolled down his cheeks, and Tammie thought she could take no more.

"He looked at me," Daniel went on. "He actually looked right into my eyes. He was half dead already, with blood running down his back - and down his face too, from some stupid crown of thorn plants they'd made him wear to mock him. He was carrying part of his cross, and stumbling about, and every time he fell they hit him and... and they laughed at him. And he looked right at me, right into my face. And I couldn't do anything. I couldn't make them stop. I wanted to rescue him. I wanted to make them kill me with him, but I couldn't even do that. So I just looked at him. And he looked at me, with so much pain and love in his eyes. And I thought my heart would break. I wish it would."

There was silence. After a long pause, Benjamin finished the story lifelessly.

"I managed to get Daniel away safely, and we left Jerusalem - I'm not sure how. We got as far as we could that day, but we had to keep hiding. We stuck out a mile; no one travels in Passover week. I was afraid we might be stopped, so when we got to the deserted parts by the River Jordan we found somewhere to hide till the holiday was over. Then we set off again, round the wilderness way, just trying to get back home."

So that was it. There was nothing more to be said. It was true that someone might have rescued Jesus, or the authorities might have changed their minds - but there had been that darkness. They all knew beyond a doubt that the darkened sky and deep, deep rumbling had marked Jesus's death.

They didn't spend a lot of time talking or trying to comfort each other. There was no comfort possible. They didn't even worry much about their loved ones still in Jerusalem, at the heart of the danger. Time had ended now, and nothing would matter ever again. They gradually split up, and everyone went to some part of the house to be alone.

Tammie found her way onto the roof. She sat in her corner gazing at the stars, sometimes just slumped there exhausted as if she could never cry or hurt or care about anything again, and sometimes breaking out afresh into a new agony of sobbing. Did God understand how she felt now? Was that how he felt, too? How, *how* could he have let it happen? The stars in the sky gave her no answers. They just twinkled coldly back at her, looking pretty. They were no help. Nothing could help.

She stayed there in the cold for the rest of the night, until at last the sky began to go a dreary grey, and the dawn was near. There was that morning star again. It had comforted her before, but now she knew what had happened. It was wasting its energy sparkling at her like that, trying to show her how to hope. Hope had gone from the world, and no bright morning star could make her think otherwise. She looked at it without caring until it faded as the sun crept over the horizon and tried to warm her with its beams.

There was a noise in the distance. She didn't care about that either, but it grew louder and she couldn't blot it out. It sounded like a bunch of partygoers, whooping and having a good time. They were probably drunk. She covered her ears against the noise; it hurt her that people could be so happy.

But it carried on getting closer and closer, so eventually she poked her head over the wall and gazed apathetically up the road out of Capernaum. There they were; a big crowd of people and donkeys and goodness knows what, laughing and dancing towards the town, waving palm leaves and brightly coloured scarves.

Tammie was about to turn away when suddenly she saw something that made her gasp. There, in the middle of the revellers,... waving to her like he was fit to bust,... was her father.

Chapter Twenty

SHINIER THAN YOUR AVERAGE GARDENER

Tammie's heart leapt, and she clung to the wall as her legs gave way beneath her. She had to get down there; she had to see her father. She broke her gaze away from that group of people and stumbled down the steps, missing nearly every other one and skinning her elbow as she went.

As she crossed the courtyard with her eyes fixed on the gate, neither hearing nor seeing anything else, others joined her. They too had seen the ecstatic group of Jesus's friends, and the pull to get out there to them was as sharp and painful as the grief had been.

They tore the bar from the gate, all fingers and thumbs, and spilled tripping over each other, out into the world again. They had cut themselves off for so many days, it was like being freed from a prison. Those left inside, amazed at their behaviour, came straggling out after them, bemused and breathless.

As they rounded the corner, the group dancing down the road caught sight of them and in an instant set off running towards them. So many old friends, their faces radiant and beaming - Jairus and his two colleagues from the Council; Salome, and Daniel's mum, and the other women - including Jesus's own mother; Simon Peter, Andrew, James and John, Thomas, Matthew and the rest of the Eleven; the man who had come through Dibs's roof, and many, many people Tammie had never seen before - from Judea, and Syria, and Africa, and Greece... Even a Roman centurion was in there, cheerily waving among the rest. Even people from *Samaria*, for goodness sake. They never usually came anywhere near Capernaum! Samaritans looked down on Judeans and Galileans nearly as much as Judeans and Galileans looked down on Samaritans. The only thing they all agreed on was wanting to kick out the Romans.

What on earth had brought this weirdly mismatched crew together, and how could they be so joyful?

"He's alive! He's alive!" they were all shouting at the top of their lungs, and the group who had emerged from Tammie's house just stood there blinking, staring helplessly at them.

When the newcomers reached them it was like being hit by a bucket of ice water, or a fresh strong wind that snatches the breath from your mouth and knocks you flying - blowing all the rubbish out of your mind and making you want to scream and shout and do cartwheels, even if you know you can't do cartwheels.

The new arrivals grabbed someone they knew (quite a few even grabbed someone they didn't know) and hugged and squeezed and kissed them, until they too were laughing hysterically through their exhaustion and wondering if the entire world had gone mad or just this bit of it. Jairus enveloped Tammie and her mother in a bear hug and lifted them off their feet, swinging them round and round and round until there was no way of knowing which way was up, let alone what could have happened. Tammie clung tightly to her father, with her nose squashed up against his armpit, and cried and laughed and spluttered snot into his tunic.

"He's alive," Jairus said when he put them down again. "He is *alive*!!!" It seemed to be all most of them were capable of saying, in the avid conversations taking place throughout the crowd.

"How?" the others were gasping. "Was there a reprieve?"

"Did you rescue him?"

"Did they cut him down before he died?"

"No no no," interrupted the centurion, who had been swapping stories with Marcellus in Latin at double speed. "He was dead; I checked."

"Of course!" said Daniel in amazement. "You were one of the soldiers who was taking him to be killed!"

"I was in charge," said the centurion, solemnly. "But there is no doubt. It was important for them that he must be seen to be dead. Very important prisoner to them. So I checked carefully. He was dead after only six hours. I know what I am doing; he was dead."

They looked round at each other with open mouths, and round at the newcomers who were beaming back at them.

"And,... he's alive now?" said Naomi, just to make sure they were following all this correctly.

"Oh yes, he's alive, he's alive," they chorused happily, going back to their favourite phrase.

"I put him into my tomb," said Jairus's friend Joseph, his face shining with joy in a way that seemed oddly moving, considering the sad things he was saying. "I plucked up all my courage to ask Pilate for the body, and he gave it me! I knew it was dangerous to let them know I supported Jesus, but I couldn't bear to think of him being left lying around for the birds and animals - or thrown into some pit with murderers and thieves. He died like a criminal, but I wanted him to be buried like a nobleman. We took him, Nicodemus and I, and bathed and anointed him, then carefully wrapped him in grave cloths and laid him inside the tomb. We thought we were saying goodbye to him! It was a preparation day for a Sabbath, of course, and dusk was near, so we couldn't take too long. Then we left him there, and a squad of soldiers moved in to guard the tomb. They thought we might steal the body and try to claim he wasn't dead! That was the last thing on our minds. Our world had ended; we couldn't have carried on without him."

"*Well*?" demanded Benjamin, hopping around with impatience. "You keep telling us he's alive, but everything you've said is about him being dead."

"Of course," said Jairus calmly, as if it were the most logical thing in the world. "He had to die first before he could be alive again, didn't he?"

"But are you sure he's alive?" persisted Benjamin.

"The tomb was empty... " began Salome.

"Maybe one of his followers did take the body," said Benjamin hopelessly. "How can we ever know?"

"Will you listen?" said Salome, who was spilling over with what she wanted to tell them. "The tomb was empty when a few of the women and I went early on the morning after the Sabbath with perfumed spices to anoint his body. The huge round stone at the entrance had been rolled to one side."

"Are you sure you went to the right tomb?" asked Rachel, trying to be helpful.

"Quite sure," said Salome firmly. "For one thing, we had watched from a distance when Joseph put him in, so we knew which one it was. And for another, there were angels in shining robes, one sitting on the stone and one inside."

There was a gasp from all who hadn't heard the

story yet, and any other objections went out of their minds.

"That's nothing," whispered Jairus, with a twinkle in his eye. "Keep listening!"

"They told us not to be afraid," laughed Salome. "We were terrified! Then the one inside the tomb showed us the place where he had been lying, with the grave cloths crumpled as if he'd just disappeared from inside them, and the headpiece all neatly folded up. He told us that Jesus had risen - risen from the dead, and that we should tell Simon Peter and the others. They thought we'd gone mad of course, but that didn't matter - because then,... " she broke off and began laughing and weeping, and squeezing Naomi's arm. "Oh, I'm sorry, my dears," she said as she wiped her eyes. "I still can't think of it... Then, oh then, we saw him. Jesus himself. Our Lord, right there in the flesh; strong and alive, and so beautiful. He was just as when we knew him, just as he used to be before he died, only more so. Much, much more so. I know I'm rambling and not making any sense, but oh, he was shining and alive and *real* - so much more alive than before he died. He was magnificent."

"You actually saw him," breathed Naomi in wonder. "You recognised that it was him."

"Yes, well no, not straightaway," said Salome, trying to collect herself and tell her story more sensibly. "My friend Mary, from Magdala across the lake, she saw him first, and she thought he was the gardener! We still didn't know what to believe - it was such a turnaround we just couldn't take it in. But when he greeted us, suddenly we saw. It was as if we had never seen clearly before in our lives. We threw ourselves at his feet and worshipped him. We just hugged his feet, and kissed and wept on them."

She embraced Naomi, and they cried with joy.

"You've actually seen him. You've touched him and talked to him," Naomi kept repeating, awestruck. "And now the other followers don't think you're mad; now they believe that what you said was true."

"They didn't really need to," said Salome. "He's appeared to most of them too."

"*What*?!!" was the general response to that.

"Oh yes," said Salome, "that was just the first time. He appeared to Simon Peter, and then the Eleven... "

"Without Thomas," cut in Jairus.

"Yes, and then the Eleven with Thomas," continued Salome. "And he had something to eat because they were afraid he was a ghost. And lots of the rest of us were there both times... "

"And our friends over there," said Joseph, pointing to two men jabbering away to Caleb, who was listening open-mouthed.

"Yes, Cleopas and... and whatsisname," said Jairus. "They were leaving Jerusalem on that first day, and Jesus caught them up and walked with them for miles without letting them see who he was. They didn't realise until they were at supper with him and he broke the bread, then he disappeared. They came tearing all the way back to Jerusalem again! By then a lot of us had seen him too. They told us that, as they walked, he taught them all sorts of things from the scriptures - about how they predicted his death, and that he would come back to life... "

"What things?" asked Tammie eagerly.

"Oh, all sorts," said Jairus, flinging his arms out in a gesture that seemed to include everything, and nearly hitting a couple of fishermen who were walking up the road and glaring at them for being in the way. "They start to pop out at you from all over."

"I wonder if he'll ever appear to anyone again," said Benjamin wistfully.

"Oh yes," said Salome, as if it were all settled - which indeed it was. "That's why we're here. It was part of the message from the angels, and from Jesus himself. Didn't I tell you?"

"No!!!" said everyone who had not been in Jerusalem, most emphatically.

"We were told to tell Peter and the others to go to Galilee, and he would meet them there."

Their mouths dropped open at this, and they all started looking over their shoulders.

"No point," smiled Jairus. "When he wants you to see him, you will, believe me. Even locked doors don't make any difference. And in the meantime, we really might as well go inside and have something to eat."

Chapter Twenty-one

HE DEFINITELY DID IT

This seemed like an excellent idea, and throughout the crowd people were realising that they had been talking in the road for a considerable time. They began breaking up, with those who lived in Capernaum busily inviting those from elsewhere to stay with them.

"Let's go somewhere we can praise God!" Tammie heard Thomas shout to a cluster of Samaritans he seemed to have adopted as best buddies. He scooped Jake up onto his shoulders, and Jakey gave his usual celebratory "Whoop-di-diddly-dooya" as Thomas trotted off arm-in-arm with his new friends. Dibs followed, rolling her eyes at Tammie; this suddenly positive - nay, exuberant - version of her uncle was going to take a bit of getting used to. There'd be no more difficulty telling him and Tobias apart.

As Tammie's house was so big, they were able to have lots of people - old friends like Joseph and Nicodemus, and new ones such as Cleopas and Whatsisname, as Rachel insisted on calling them. It was like a rolling celebration, and though work still had to be done, they made opportunities to meet together as much as possible. Other supporters of Jesus drifted in too, having heard of the instruction to go to Galilee, and soon there were about five hundred of them in total - stashed away in houses all over the town. Everywhere the atmosphere was charged with excitement, and his followers were brimming over with joy. Except one.

Tammie noticed it quite early on, probably because she always noticed where Daniel was and how he was feeling. He joined in the celebrating as much as he could, but he would often slink off as if it were too much for him.

A few days after the resurrection party had rocked up, Tammie saw him leave again and slipped out after him. She so much wanted him to be happy. She looked around and spotted him at a distance, sitting on the shoreline of the lake. Rather shyly she went over, and since he looked up and gave a little smile, she sat down next to him. They watched the lake lapping quietly at their feet, hearing the singing of their friends rejoicing once more at a distance.

Eventually Daniel gave a sigh and looked at her.

"I do believe it, you know," he said. "I really do believe that he's alive. It's not that."

He looked back at the lake, and Tammie waited for him to continue.

"I can't forget, that's all," he said after a moment. "Even though I know he's alive now, and everything's all right again, I can't forget what he looked like that last time I saw him." Tears welled up in his eyes, and he brushed them away impatiently. "Everyone is so happy, and I just can't feel the same. I feel wrong for being so sad, but I can't help it. When they say his name, I see him as he was then and it wrenches me apart, even though I know he's not like that now." He looked up at her, his eyelashes glistening. "Oh Tam, he was so bruised and hurting, as if the sadness of the whole world was weighing him down. I can't forget that look in his eyes, and the pain he was in. It's haunting me, and I just can't get rid of it."

Tammie wondered what to say that could comfort him. She couldn't think of anything, so she just touched his hand timidly.

144

"You don't feel as if you *need* to see him, do you?" Daniel asked her.

"Well no," she said. "I'd really like to, of course, but if I don't see him, I'll just believe. But then - I didn't see him the way you did."

"I feel as if I've got to see him desperately," said Daniel. "I do believe what they've told us... "

"I know you do," said Tammie. "And so does Jesus. He loves you. I'm sure he'll give you whatever you truly need."

She talked to God about it that night, and again whenever she could the next day - and when, early one morning shortly afterwards, she recognised Daniel's voice bellowing her name, she thanked God for answering before she even heard what Daniel had to say.

"Tam!! Tammie!" he yelled, and she dropped her breakfast and raced to the wall of the roof to shush him.

He scrambled up the steps, his eyes gleaming.

"Oh Tam, I've seen him!"

She didn't bother to ask who.

"Where? Did he speak to you?"

"You're joking, - we had breakfast with him! You won't believe how long we were together."

"Calm down and tell me!"

"Yesterday evening I was with my brothers, and Simon Peter and a few others, and Peter suggested we should take the boat and go fishing. We often used to fish at night in the old times, before Jesus came, and it seemed like a good idea."

He paused for breath, and grinned his old grin again. "It didn't seem so great a little while before dawn. We hadn't caught anything; not a single fish all night. Then we saw this guy on the shore... "

"Jesus," said Tammie with satisfaction.

"Yes, but we didn't know that. He called to us, asking if we'd caught anything. So we had to admit that we hadn't."

"Which he knew anyway," said Tammie.

"Then he shouted, 'Throw your nets over the other side of the boat.'"

"Huh?" laughed Tammie. "What difference would that make?"

"Exactly. Daft, or what?" said Daniel, shaking his head at the memory. "So we hauled the net in and transferred it to the other side, and of course, you can guess what happened."

"Lots of fish."

"A hundred and fifty three, to be precise. Real whoppers, too."

"You *counted* them?"

"Later, yes. We had to; we just couldn't believe it! And the net hadn't torn even a little bit. It was amazing. Anyway, John guessed straight off it was Jesus, and Peter jumped over the side to go and greet him while we all brought the boat in, towing the net. There was no way we could have lifted it into the boat! And there he was - strong and full of life, just like Salome said. And he'd made us breakfast! There was a fire there on the beach for us to warm ourselves, and he was cooking some bread and fish. I can't tell you how awesome it tasted, and how I felt as we sat there and talked with him for ages."

"So did you tell him he's not that amazing, coming back to life?" teased Tammie.

"No way! He looks completely new. Kind of like him, but you can tell it's not the same body. You and those others were just lent a bit more time - put back into your old, imperfect bodies for however many years longer. But Jesus looks like he'll be alive forever."

Tammie hadn't thought of it that way before. "So I get to die twice. Thanks for pointing that out."

"I suppose we've all got to face it. At least you've already done it - you know you don't need to be afraid. Wow! You're miles ahead of the rest of us," said Daniel. He smiled again, remembering Jesus. "Though I don't feel as if I can be scared of anything right now."

Tammie grinned back at him, her eyes sparkling in answer to his.

"Everyone will be so excited he's been seen again," she said. "We must make sure they all know."

"Yes, of course," Daniel said with a start, suddenly remembering. "That's why I came here. We all split up to call a meeting at Peter's house this afternoon, to tell about this latest appearance. I said I'd bring the message here, so that I could see you."

Their eyes happened to meet as he said that, and they both looked away hastily and both went their usual shade of purple in face or ear - though as they weren't looking at each other it didn't really matter. Daniel hurriedly thought of something else to say.

"There's more good news, too. Jesus has shown Simon Peter that he's still the leader of the Eleven and the rest of us. He couldn't forget the way he let Jesus down, but now Jesus has shown how much he forgives him, he can't not forgive himself, can he? You should see Peter now; he's so confident and strong - you'll hardly know him."

It was true. When Tammie sat listening to him that afternoon on the shoreline outside his house, he had all the ease of a practised public speaker. You would never have believed he was an ordinary fisherman, with no more education than the scriptural bits and pieces all the boys were given. The lumbering bear of a man who rarely spoke, and the impulsive disciple with a tendency to put his foot in it, were toned down and blended - and what had grown from them was a tall, wise man, full of grace and good teaching.

They all listened rapt as Peter spoke, explaining the events of the past few weeks and pointing to the greater meaning in scripture. He showed them how Jesus's victory hadn't been over an ordinary, human enemy, but over death itself; it somehow wasn't the end anymore. Jesus had died their death for them and had given them his perfection - like a straight swap, if they chose to take it. This meant that they could be with God again, forever, just like it was meant to be in the first place.

"Nicodemus has something to tell us about this," said Simon Peter, inviting Nicodemus to the front.
"Yes," said Nicodemus, clearing his throat. "As you know, I am a member of the Sanhedrin, the Council in Jerusalem, and before we came away I heard a rumour which was going around my colleagues. I found it to be true, although the chief priests were trying to stop the story. You all know of the curtain which hangs in the Temple, to separate the Holy place from the Most Holy Place, where God dwells. At the very moment when Jesus died, when the earthquake shook the city - that curtain was ripped in two, and nobody knows how."

Tammie leaped to her feet yelling "*HE DID IT!!!*" at the very top of her voice, and was immediately dragged down again by Naomi and Rachel, who were sitting on either side of her. People turned to her, aghast: not exactly angry, but beyond surprised. Nicodemus looked at Simon Peter, not sure what to do; Simon Peter looked at Tammie, who was wishing that she had never been born and that the ground would open up in front of her and provide a handy chasm into which she could throw herself and prevent further embarrassment to her friends and relations.

"What do you mean by 'He did it'?" asked Peter calmly, as if comments - in the form of loud shrieks - had been invited from the floor. Perhaps he saw something of himself in her enthusiasm.

"Nothing," mumbled Tammie, trying to telescope her spine into itself to make her as small as she actually felt.

"No, I'm serious Tammie," he continued. "What was the point you were making?"

He seemed interested rather than cross, and her father nodded to her not to be afraid. She stood shakily to her feet. Emigration to a distant part of Africa seemed the best plan.

"Well," she stammered, wondering what on earth to say. "Once I talked with Jesus about the curtain, and now he's actually done it. I mean... What I'm trying to say is - that curtain was there to separate us from God, and now he's died for us it's been ripped open, so we can go straight to God and be with him again... That's it, really."

She slipped thankfully to the ground again, and an approving murmur rippled round the listeners. Dibs poked her head round Rachel, eyebrows raised, with a very impressed look. Tammie gave a sigh of relief. Maybe she wouldn't go to live in Africa.

"Excellent," said Nicodemus. "Our young friend has caught hold of something very important here."

He went on explaining further what Tammie had said, putting it into tidier and more theological language, and Tammie listened with pleasure. The time went by with more from Simon Peter and others, and them all joining in the prayer Jesus had taught them (which Tammie had first heard as an audience of one to Daniel's re-enactment on the banks of the Korazin).

There was lots of Psalm singing too, as they all came to see what amazing things God had planned to do for them right from the start. They truly believed this was the fulfilment of everything their ancestors had been waiting for over so many centuries - and now here they were, actually living through it!

It was all too much for Tammie. She was so happy, and proud of Jesus, and full of love for God, she just had to be on her own for a little while. She slipped away quietly and cut around the outskirts of the town. She knew just where she wanted to go.

What was going to happen, she couldn't tell. Life could never go on as it had. Her father would not be allowed to keep his place in the synagogue, or on the Council; some of their number, like Marcellus and his friend, were in danger of losing more than just their job. But how could she doubt that God had it all under his control, when she had seen the wonderful things he had done for them?

Whatever happened, Jesus was with them now, and could never be taken away. Nor could anyone try to keep God's love from them. She made her way to the olive grove and stayed there for a while - where, an eternity ago, she had walked in the cool of the evening with her friend Jesus.

21103888R00095

Printed in Great Britain
by Amazon